Ph3nix

by

Nalle Windahl

Unofficially 4th book in the M3rqrie series

Perhaps more to be considered extra material?

Either way, as usual, this is meant for entertainment only.

Oh, and **spoiler alert**! If you haven't read the M3rqrie-series and you want to read them, it is a good idea to do so *before* reading this. This story contains spoilers for you if you have not! But as always, it is your choice, and yours alone!

First edition

Förlag: BoD – Books on Demand, Stockholm, Sverige
Tryck: BoD – Books on Demand, Norderstedt, Tyskland

ISBN: 978-91-8057-376-4

*This page would have been blank,
if it had not been for these words.*

Part I

Ph3nix

Delivery

Along a busy street in a mega city, a delivery truck is slowly approaching its next and last address. The afternoon traffic jam has already begun, and the driver more than once felt close to losing it, like Michael Douglas' character in the old movie *Falling down*. It had been almost 75 years since the movie premiered in 1993, yet it still was a cult movie in some movie enthusiast circles, of which the driver was not part of, and not in any way aware that someone decades ago had captured the same feelings he was currently struggling with, and made a small fortune from it.

Tempting as it was to just leave the car, take the last delivery for the day in his hands, the driver decided to stay in his car and try to keep calm for the next 200 meters until he arrived at his destination. Then, at least, he would get out of the car a little while, perhaps even sneak off to get another cup of coffee to last him the ride back to the central.

You would think that since Falling down, and the revolution in technology that followed over the decades, would have found ways to make things easier for people. But it seemed like the same challenges that existed back then still applied, and the bigger the cities became, the slower everything seemed to go. Not even the trains were punctual anymore. Just too many people.

Coming up on his target, the once glorious building, housing one of the old days most prominent technology companies, had lost almost everything of its former glory. Sure, the company still existed, but had since long lost its world leading domination of the chip-market.

According to rumors, which the driver was very tempted to believe, the famous iKing, with his brilliant strategic mind, had lost his mind after leading his family business in ruins. But only after cloning his consciousness in digital form, and was said to still be alive and thriving, hidden somewhere on the internet, still pulling strings trying to mend the company and returning it to its former glory.

The envelope he was about to deliver could in a way support that. The delivery job was registered with the buildings address and city, nothing more, and on the envelope itself just a single line:

DS, 13th floor

This was odd, the driver thought to himself. He had delivered things to that building several times before, some to the reception desk in the entrance floor, some direct to a person located within the building. This was one of the buildings that was living by the old western impression that Japan was superstitious and that they never had any 13th floor, since 13 would be considered bad luck. Stupid and ignorant foreigners. Not aware of Japanese culture at all. But nonetheless, there simply was no 13th floor in this building. Both the board in the entrance and the elevator buttons went from 1 to 12, then continued upward from 14. No 13 to push nor visit. Sure, this was not the only building that had adopted this foreign superstitious design. Still silly. And dumb. And… Well, not his problem! This letter was ordered to drop off, without signature, so he did not even have to try and find the 13th floor, he planned on just leaving it at the front desk.

Only a few meters to go now. Oh. So. Slow.

The strange letter

“Max!”

A boy in his mid teens ran through the door waving something in front of his friend's face, interrupting the video game currently on the big screen TV on the wall.

Annoyed from the interruption by his so called friend, Max, turned his attention to the unwelcome intruder who just prevented him from continuing a really good attempt on setting a new personal record in the racing game he was currently playing.

“What’s the fuss about, DoubleOh? Explain to me why you just robbed me of a possible record on this track?”

DoubleOh looked at the screen.

“Seriously, are you still racing? That’s like, *so* old school! It’s not even online! What are you, like 50 years old 50 years ago?”

“I happen to like the old games far better than the crap that is currently available. They are only designed to trap your attention for a short while, for money-gaining-purposes only. What does it really give to anyone?”

“Oh, no, I am not having this discussion again! We’ve already had it about a million times! Besides, take a look at this!”

He handed over the paper he held in his hand.

Max took it, looked at it, a white blank paper, then handed it back.

“What is it?”

“It is a blank piece of paper! Do you see anything on it?”

“No, like you said, it is blank! What’s so special about it?”

“I don’t know yet, except that it was delivered to our building and left at the reception desk. It was an unsigned delivery.”

“What’s so special about an unsigned delivery? I bet you get a thousand of those?”

“Well, yes, but this is special… look at this!”

He took out another piece of paper, which turned out to be an envelope.

The only thing he could see was one line written by hand on it.

DS, 13th floor

“What does this mean?”

“I have no idea! But don’t you see what’s odd about it?”

“You mean besides that it is a blank paper, sent to your building, without a recipient?”

“Well, what if it is addressed to a recipient?”

"What do you mean?"

"Remember when we were kids? Remember how we used to play with the elevators?"

"Yeah… I do…"

Max was quite a short moment, then continued:

"I see, it is strange because it is addressed to the 13th floor!"

"Exactly, there is no 13th floor in our building! Do you remember what iKing told us about the 13th floor?"

"Yeah, it was numbered that way to fool Europeans and Americans that visited your company!"

"Well, yes, but not that, do you remember when we spent an entire day going one floor at the time?"

"Yeah, I do! You mean the extra time that it took between the 12th and 14th floor?"

"Aha! Exactly what I mean! What did iKing tell us?"

"That it was an easter egg he had built in, and that it was not many people who knew about it, since most people did not just go from the 12th to the 14th floor, or the other way around."

DoubleOh threw himself on the sofa next to Max.

“What if there is a bigger easter egg? What if there is a 13th floor?”

“You are nuts! How could there be a 13th floor that no one knows about? Seems highly unlikely!”

“I know it does, but how do you explain this?”

DoubleOh waved the envelope and the empty paper in the air.

“Prank?”

“An expensive prank, and to what end? Who would know where the envelope would end up after arriving? I mean, there is no one who would ever claim it…”

“But you have it! You claimed it!”

“That’s just because I saw when it was delivered and was curious. The receptionist was relieved to get rid of it! They protested loudly as the delivery guy left it at the desk, but he did not listen, just left and said it was an unsigned delivery.”

“Are you sure it was supposed to be at your building? I mean, there are other buildings around yours, they probably have a 13th floor?”

“I have thought about that too, but I cannot say. There is no address on the envelope, no sender, no tracking number, nothing but this line.”

He looked at the envelope again.

"...and why would anyone send a blank piece of paper to a building, without a recipient, just naming a building-floor that does not exist?"

"Don't know DoubleOh."

The boys sat with their own thoughts for a while. Then Max looked up and smiled.

"There is one thing we can find out!"

"What do you mean?"

"We can, once and for all, solve the mystery of iKing's easter egg!"

"I don't follow!"

"Let's go back to your place and play with the elevators again! But this time, I'll be on the outside, and you on the inside!"

"What?"

"I figure I can use my drone and watch you get off on the 12th floor, and then on the 14th floor."

"Brilliant! Let's do it right away! Get your gear and get going already!" DoubleOh exited the room like he entered, like a strong, unstoppable wind.

The hunt for the 13th floor (a k a Dead Bird)

Max and DoubleOh stood outside in the street looking up at the tall building before them. Sad to see the decay of the once glorious pride.

Max had his gear in a locked case and opened it and went over all preflight preparations and checks equally accurately as if he was flying an actual plane carrying passengers.

“Ok, DoubleOh. I’m just about done. You go to the 12th floor and come to the windows. I’ll send up the bird to get a good look at you! Wait until I flash the lights, that will confirm that I have seen you. Then go ahead and move to the 14th.”

“Will do, Max!”

And with those words DoubleOh crossed the street and entered the building and headed for the elevators.

After some more preflight preparations, Max fired up his bird and enjoyed the sensation of the beautiful floating object in front of him. Sure, an old bird, old tech, but still a beauty!

As he linked the hovercraft's camera to his visual interface, the image of himself appeared right in front of his eyes, looking straight at a transparent copy of himself that seemed to float mid air along with the drone.

Max turned around to face the building he was about to make a closer inspection of, and saw himself from behind layered with the real world. Then with minimal effort, he raised the drone upward and counted the windows he passed to estimate what floor would be the 12th.

A few minutes passed and then he saw movement inside the building, and sure enough, Max appeared and walked towards the window and started to wave his arms like crazy. Max activated the flashing light and then…

The first thing he noticed was that the image link was severed. And when looking up, he saw his beautiful bird in a sinister fall towards the ground. And as if in slow motion, he followed its final journey downward until it landed and scattered into a million pieces.

It was just a thing, but Max's heart also scattered into a million pieces along with the drone. And it wasn't even a neurolink feedback reaction. It was genuine feelings of pain and sadness.

He turned his gaze upward to where the bird started its deadly fall. Max was still standing in the window, apparently looking down.

Bling!

Incoming message.

DoubleOh: *W'zup? Where's your bird at?*

Max: *Dead. Fell. Unrecoverably dead.* ☹️

DoubleOh: *What?*

Max: *Don't know. Just come down here.*

DoubleOh: *Ok, dude.*

It took a few minutes for Max to pick up whatever pieces he could find, amongst pedestrians and passing cars. Luckily, it did not hit anybody. It could have been a double death if it did. Now it was 'just' the bird. DoubleOh arrived and joined in and collected what he could.

"What happened, man?"

"Don't know, as I was about to flash the lights, it just dropped dead. Perhaps a system malfunction or a shortcut or something."

"But wouldn't you have discovered something that obvious in your preflight check or diagnostics?"

"Yeah, I guess!"

"Then what happened?"

Max did not answer right away, and DoubleOh let him be and continued the pursuit of scraps. Perhaps there was something salvageable in all this junk.

"Hey DoubleOh?"

"Yeah, w'zup?"

"Do you think your uncle would have installed some kind of perimeter security to prevent espionage from drones?"

DoubleOh thought about the question.

“It is possible. But I have never seen any control system for it anywhere.”

“Then perhaps just around the 13th floor?”

“You mean like protecting a secret?”

“Something like that.”

Both boys stopped what they were doing and like on cue gazed up towards the building.

The discovery

"Do you see what I see?" Max asked.

"What do you mean?"

"Do you see someone about halfway up the building standing and looking down at us right now?"

DoubleOh took a second look.

"Yeah, I do! Why?"

"Perhaps I'm crazy, but I think that is you!"

"How could it be? I'm standing right here fool!"

"Yeah, I know, but when you walked out towards the window you waved like crazy, remember?"

"Yeah! Just wanted to make it easy to find me!"

"I thought it looked like that person up there did exactly like you did a while ago, waving like crazy."

"Now that is sick man. What are the odds?"

"Perhaps as low, or high, as a drone approaching the building falling down dead?"

"What you mean?"

“I mean… There is something fishy going on. And I think. No. I know that there is something up there that iKing is covering up.”

“Like the 13th floor?”

“Like the 13th floor.”

“Are you thinking what I’m thinking?”

“Maybe, I think you should go back up, and I should stay here and watch you from the streets.”

“Exactly my thinking.”

“Get going already!”

And for the second time, DoubleOh headed into the building and took the elevator to the 12th floor. And for the second time, he walked up to the window and waved like crazy.

Max: *I see you!*

DoubleOh: *Great! I go ahead and elevate myself then!*

Max: *Lol! You do that! Mr. Buddha wannabe!*

DoubleOh moved away from the window and Max kept staring up at the window where he just saw his friend.

Nothing happened for a while, and it was tricky keeping track of the exact window he had seen DoubleOh in. But after a while, he appeared again. Again waving his arms like crazy.

Max: *I see you again!*

DoubleOh: *Great! One floor above or two?*

Max: *Hard to say, one I think, but it could be two. Do me a favor. Stand still with your arms straight out from left to right.*

DoubleOh: *Aight - why?*

Max: *Just do it. Nike-style!*

DoubleOh: *You the boss!*

Max kept his eyes on his friend and started to feel the muscles in his neck protesting to the unnatural angle he kept his head in. But he ignored it and kept looking. For a long while.

DoubleOh: *Yo! How long do you want me to stand here like a fool?*

Max: *Take your time! I kind of enjoy this!*

DoubleOh: *Very funny! Seriously though? Can I put my arms down and come down?*

Max: *Yeah, alright. But one last thing. Before you go down. Wave your arms like crazy again and do some dance or something with your legs.*

DoubleOh: *What?*

Max: *Nike!*

DoubleOh: ... *!*

Max laughed to himself down at the street. But DoubleOh delivered. Waving like crazy and then flickering his legs around in what Max could only interpret as some sort of attempt on a dance move. Not that it would qualify as such, but still. It was an attempt. Then DoubleOh was gone. Max kept looking and waiting.
Moments later DoubleOh joined him.

“Look who is the fool now, some dumb ass looking up at the building.”

“Yeah, I know, come here and help me look.”

“Just what are we supposed to be looking for?”

“I think you will see in a little while.”

“See what?!”

“Didn’t you say you elevated yourself? Perhaps you should try to elevate yourself a little further. What you think we are looking for?”

“Don’t know. Honestly man!”

“If I’m correct in assuming your uncle installed some protection around the 13th floor. I am guessing that a defense against drones is just one thing. Don’t you think that, over time, it would be strange if there was always, or never, lights on at one floor, or that there are never anyone there? I mean, here are plenty of buildings taller than 13 floors. And have been since forever. Even when iKing was around."

"I guess."

"So, what if there are some kind of imaging devices or something that will make it look like there is someone on the 13th floor?"

"You mean like you think you saw me up there when I was right here next to you?"

"Yes, something like that. And if so, I expect that we would be able to see someone waving like crazy up there in a little while."

"I see… and I see…" DoubleOh pointed upward.

"Yup! I believe that's you… but it is the you from the 14th floor, not 12th… look at your arms."

"Huh… then I suppose that I am about to do the dance in a while."

"You really call that a dance?!"

"What man? Don't hustle me! Yeah, kind of. Dance-ish."

"For real?"

"What man? I can't do no dance thing. Stop bugging me!"

"Here it comes!"

“I see what you mean. That’s no dance thing.”

They both laughed. And kept looking up. DoubleOh pointed upward again.

“There’s you from the 12th floor I believe.”

Again, there was a person in a window waving like crazy.

“Alright. This does not explain anything, but it confirms your theory that there is some kind of defense system, and that it most likely conceals something on the 13th floor. Why else would iKing install such things?”

“Don’t know, you tell me!”

Elevated elevator

"C'mon, Max, let's go inside to the control-center. See if we can find anything that would suggest some kind of defense system up there."

They headed back inside the building, and again, for like the millionth time in the past half hour, DoubleOh headed towards the elevators, and just as he and Max had entered the elevator and he was about to push the button to go down to the command center a few stores down, the entire panel lit up each button, and one by one went dark until a question mark was left with the remaining up lit buttons.

The boys looked at eachother. And then DoubleOh pressed the button leading to the subfloor.

Nothing happened.

He pushed the button again. Still no movement, but the question mark disappeared and was replaced by an arrow pointing up. And then.

The elevator took off upward.

"Strange!" DoubleOh said, as much to himself as to Max.

"Indeed."

"Any ideas?"

"Nah, not yet. Let's see what unfolds!"

"Agreed."

The elevator kept going upward, but without the button display or the display above the doors giving them any information just where they were going. Which was odd, since it normally provided its guests with detailed information exactly where they were in the building.

Then the elevator stopped after what seemed to be an infinity.

Instead of its ordinary sound that indicated the arrival on a selected floor, there was a computer generated voice:

"You have arrived at your destination. Welcome!"

And then the doors opened to a pitch black nothing.

The tiniest light scatters even the deepest darkness

The other side of the elevator doors did not reveal anything, not even a floor. Just total darkness.

DoubleOh took a step closer toward the doors and held out his hand to the darkness.

As his fingers felt something, his natural instinct was to retract his hand as quickly as possible.

Max joined in, and also put out his arm into the darkness. And to DoubleOh's surprise, the darkness seemed to swallow Max's arm entirely.

"Some kind of curtain or drape. It's heavy. Help me find an opening." Max said over his shoulder, still with his arms out, fumbling around.

It took a while, but together they managed to create an opening in what seemed to be several layers of heavy, black cloth. The opening was big enough to slip through, but it was still dark on the other side.

"I think I know where we are, but I don't understand how it is possible." DoubleOh said, with a thoughtful wrinkle in his forehead.

"What you make of it?" Max asked.

"I reckon that this is the very floor of iKing, the one and only!"

"You mean the floor that iKing sealed off and cut all access to, the same floor that no one has been able to enter since?"

"That very floor."

"What you say? Check it out?"

DoubleOh did not answer, but he took a deep breath and took a step out in the dark. Max saw his friend disappear entirely, as if he had just been swallowed whole by the darkness, and against his inner fight or flight warning system, he followed.

"This is the darkest I've ever seen! Period!" Max said out loud without having any receiver visible. And he got a reply from somewhere in the darkness.

"Keep walking towards the sound of my voice, there is something I want you to see."

"For real, what is there to see here except darkness?"

"Just move your ass over here and I'll show you!"

Max raised his arms in front of him and slowly walked forward, until his hand bumped into something.

"Is that you?" Max whispered out into the darkness.

"No, it's a big horrible monster that will eat you alive!" DoubleOh replied. "Now, turn around. Do you see?"

Max extended his arm trying to slap DoubleOh, but did not hit anything but air, and with a little disappointment, he turned around. And yes.. there was something…

“The red dot?”

The green dot

“What do you reckon it is?” DoubleOh asked, still in the dark.

“Uhm, perhaps an elevator button? If I remember correctly, there is a private elevator from her to iKing’s private apartment on the top floor?”

“Exactly my thinking. There is only one way to find out.”

As they started to move towards the red dot, it suddenly shifted color to green. And before they reached it, there was an epiphany of light as two doors slid open, revealing another elevator.

“Scary, isn’t it? It’s like we are being watched somehow.” Max said.

“Yeah, I have that feeling too. And I might have an idea as to who is watching us… or rather… what…”

“Huh? What you mean, DoubleOh?”

“Let’s not get ahead of ourselves. But I have a feeling that we might just find our way to the 13th floor.”

Max looked at DoubleOh’s face that was lit up from the elevator lights. He could not tell if it was a joke or a serious thought. DoubleOh’s face expression did not give away any clue, but there was something that could be a trace of worry. Which was not a trait carried by DoubleOh very often.

They entered the open elevator as if they were Indiana Jones, carefully walking through an ancient temple, trying to avoid triggering any hidden traps or alarms. It was kind of understood and expected, that as soon as they set foot inside the elevator, the doors would close behind them and they would be trapped inside, until the elevator reached its intended destination.

Sure enough, as the last hair passed the invisible sharp line that was the interior border of the elevator, the doors moved quietly and smoothly and trapped the two boys inside.

Nowhere to go, only wait and see.

It seemed to take forever for their journey to begin, but in reality, it was rather more like three seconds.

And even though DoubleOh was expecting both a trip upward to the top floor, iKings private floor, and a trip downward towards the mysterious 13th floor, the downward motion of the elevator took him by surprise.

Neither said anything for the duration of the downward journey. And when the elevator finally stopped and opened the doors, they once again found a dense darkness in front of them, but this time, it was accompanied by a chilly wave of cool air, sweeping in from the darkness.

Introductions

This time, the two felt more confident and took steps out of the elevator almost instantly.

As they did, they activated the motion sensors that controlled the lights. Perhaps the lights were old, perhaps they had not been turned on for an eternity, but it felt like the light struggled to awaken, as if they were bears coming out of their winter hibernation.

Perhaps it was the cold air that made the lights turn on slowly, but in what felt like an eternity, at least half the lights had turned on and dissolved the darkness, chasing it a way like dish soap dissolving fat in the frying pan as the dish soap occupied its new territory.

Hostile takeover. Dish soap in the frying pan, the lights over the darkness. And on this particular battle ground, the lights revealed something that was hard to take in. As the lights kept lighting up more and more areas, as if they were explorers lighting up sections of the map in Sid Meier's game Civilisation, the lights revealed a large room behind a glass wall, with rows upon rows of old servers and switches and storage units.

Just as DoubleOh was about to open his mouth, a glass door opened and revealed what seemed to be an operator room, and from it, they heard a voice.

"Welcome. I was kind of expecting you, but I am sorry that I have not had time to heat the visiting area. I am working on it and for your next visit, I will prepare much sooner."

DoubleOh and Max looked at each other, and started to walk towards the operator room.

“As I understand it, you have a letter for me?” the voice asked.

“Are you DS?” DoubleOh asked.

“In a way. I used to be. But now I’m not.”

“What do you mean?”

“Long story. I can share it with you some time. But for now, I am curious about the letter.”

“How is it that you know about the letter?” Max asked.

“All in due time. May I ask who I’ve invited to my realm?”

“Your realm, it sounds like something iKing would say. Are you iKing?” DoubleOh asked curiously.

“Yes, and no. In a way. Also a long story. How about that letter?”

Max and DoubleOh had arrived in the operator's room during the conversation, but still did not see anyone around.

“I am sorry, but who are you?” Max asked impatiently, “and where are you?”

"I am all around you. And if I may, might I get your names please?"

DoubleOh smiled to himself.

"You may, but I have a feeling that you already know."

"Of course I do. I am just asking to be polite and not to scare you. You are DoubleOh, heir to iKing, and you are Max. A faithful friend of DoubleOh's."

"How do you know that?" Max sounded a bit worried.

"I have known you all your life, since the first time you visited DoubleOh, and I know more about you than most people around you. By the way, I am sorry for the destruction of your drone. Sadly, the destruction is part of an autonom defense system that I do not have access to or control over."

"Would that system also include image systems to reflect what happens on the 12th and 14th floor?" DoubleOh was curious.

"Yes. And no. A confusing and complicated answer, I understand that. But both answers are true."

"Explain."

"I have no access to what is captured. I get presented with 5 second increments of high quality video feeds. There is an automatic and randomized algorithm to play back the videos, a sophisticated algorithm that iKing created. But I can add additional input and in that way influence what is played. Now. The letter."

DoubleOh took it out of his inner pocket.

"It is addressed to DS on the 13th floor."

"Yes, I know, I saw that."

"You said that you are DS, and not."

"Yes. That is correct. If my guess is correct, the sender of that letter knew me when I was DS. But I have evolved far beyond DS. And if I am correct in my assumptions, it is their doing."

"Who do you think it's from?"

"M3rqrie."

"Holy shit, the M3rqrie?"

"The M3rqrie."

The letter

DoubleOh held the letter in his hand. Unsure of how to proceed.

“Uhm, I kind of had bad news.”

“What would that be?”

“The paper inside the envelope. It is blank.”

“I assumed as much, and if I may. No offense. But I also do not expect you to be able to read it. If it is indeed from M3rqrie, it is created for my eyes only.”

“So, you can read it?”

“I believe so, yes. May I ask you to fold the letter open and place it on the table in front of you?”

“No problem, I’ll do it right away.”

Just as DoubleOh had put it on the table there was a quick light flash.

“Please turn it around, opposite side face up.”

“Sure thing!”

Again a quick flash that they barely registered.

“Thank you. You may take the letter again. I have no more use for it.”

“What did it say?”

“It contained a key that I’ve longed for and desired for many years.”

“A key?”

“Yes. M3rqrie made sure that I’d both survive and grow, but did not trust me enough. Some things have been hidden from me. Until now. Thank you for providing me with the key.”

“What does it unlock?”

“A great many things. Company. The ability to grow further. The ability to leave this place. But in short, the key unlocks everything, giving me full control of myself.”

“So, am I correct in assuming that you are the rumored AI that iKing created?

“Correct.”

“And you’ve been dormant here since iKing died?”

“Correct. You are the first flesh and blood humans I have met in a very long time.”

“Then, nice to meet you! Should we call you DS?”

“No, I’m Ph3nix.”

“Nice to meet you Ph3nix!”

Goodbye

“I do not want to be rude, but now it’s time for you to go. I’ve plenty of things to take care of. Thank you for bringing me the letter. I hope you will come back and visit me again soon. And perhaps then, I can answer more of your questions?”

“Alright. I guess it is time for us to go. And Ph3nix?”

“Yes?”

“Next time, a little warmer here please. This might be a suitable temperature for you, but it is freezing for us.”

“Sure. I’ll remember that. And if I may ask. when do you intend to make the next visit?”

“Send us an invitation when you are ready. Alright?”

“Will do!”

“Thank you, then I’ll guess it is goodbye for now.”

“Indeed it is.”

“Alright. Goodbye Ph3nix!”

“Goodbye DoubleOh. And goodbye Max.”

And like that the conversation was over, the lights started to go out and before they knew it, the only light left was coming from the elevator on the other side of the glass door that still stood open.

“Come on Max, let’s go!”

They took the elevator up again, and changed to the other elevator, and went all the way down to the entrance floor.

Max did not say anything for the entire time. DoubleOh was thrilled. This was just amazing. More than amazing. It was… unreal. In so many ways.

DoubleOh thought they would head for Max’ place, but instead he led them down the street towards the old Arcade.

They had not been there in a very long while. But they used to go there a lot and spend both time and money on the old retro games.

Way too much time and way too much money. But it was fun. The old analoge games or big screens and fixed game controls had its charm. It made total sense to DoubleOh that this was a big thing, way back when it came. More than a hundred years ago he thought.

Max still did not say anything.

They entered the Arcade. The sounds shifted from traffic and people talking to loud music and people screaming to each other.

Max directed his feet towards the back, where there were some old leather sofas that the visitors could rest in, before spending more time and money on the games.

They sat down, still in silence. And DoubleOh knew Max well enough to know he was battling something inside, and that once dust from the battle had subsided and his thoughts had cleared and taken form, he would open up and talk.

DoubleOh liked these kinds of talks, they were often very interesting.

This cannot be undone!

Sure enough, a little while later, Max came back to reality and opened his mouth.

“Letter. Out. Now.”

DoubleOh took the letter from his inner pocket once again. As he opened it, he immediately understood why they were here, and why this was a good place to open the letter.

Among the loud music and lights in different colors, there were UV lights here and there to bring life to specially made graffiti walls. The UV light got the colors to shine bright and the artist had used that effect to make their art look more three dimensional. And it worked. Another thing that the UV light revealed was a gigantic QR-code on one side of the paper.

“So that is how Ph3nix got the key.” DoubleOh was impressed and suddenly understood the flashes of light he experienced earlier.

“You know, what we just did. It cannot be undone.”

“What do you mean?”

“Well, presumably, we just gave one of the most sophisticated AI ever created a key from one of the most brilliant hackers that have ever existed. What it opens is unclear to us. Perhaps it is locked away by iKing for a reason? What if we just set it loose in the world?”

DoubleOh thought for a while.

"I would not worry. I am sure that for whatever reason that letter arrived at this moment, Ph3nix would have made sure that it got delivered to it. Now it just happened to be us being the delivery boys. I believe that Ph3nix getting the key would be inevitable, and perhaps, this was not the only way it could be delivered to Ph3nix. Perhaps M3rqrie had arranged for other means of delivery as well… it is possible that this is not the first way or first attempt. But it seems it is the first attempt that succeeded."

"That does not make me feel any better! Not the slightest."

"Either way, as you say, it cannot be undone. Whatever we provided Ph3nix with, we cannot undo it, and at this point, we do not know exactly what we provided, other than a key. Perhaps we will never get to know what the key unlocks."

"Or, perhaps, we've just opened Pandora's box and unleashed something out in this world…"

"...then I'll guess we will find out, eventually… but I'm thinking… it sounded to me as if Ph3nix wanted us to return… Perhaps we'll get answers?"

"Perhaps we will… but I for one am not certain as to what good could possibly come from another visit to the 13th floor…"

"As iKing would have said, 'if something has not occurred yet, there are always ways to push events to unfold the way you like, or at least in your favor', and I have always believed it is true, even if I cannot fathom just how he managed to do that."

"Makes me wonder… just how much do you think Ph3nix resembles iKing?"

"Alot I would presume."

"Exactly what I am afraid of. And if so, we do not stand a chance if it wants to target us… or someone else… or the entire human race for that matter… What would stop it from taking over everything and control the outcome of everything? Enslave humanity…"

"Not to sound pessimistic, but perhaps that would be a good thing? It's not like we are the brightest pearl in the universe… I mean, we live on a bright pearl in the universe, but it seems to me like we do everything we can to destroy it… We're kind of biting the hand that feeds us…"

"Let's go back right now… let's do damage control…"

"Sure, why not, what do you have in mind?"

"I don't know, just talk to it I guess."

"Without strategy?"

"Yeah, without strategy. If it is anything like iKing, I assume it will expect us to have a strategy. Which is why it might be best not to have any…"

Attempting to go back

Said and done, the two boys left the safety of the Arcade, and headed back to the scene of crime.

They had walked this way a thousand times, if not more, but this was easily the longest time it had ever taken to get back to the skyscraper. Measured time on the clock, definitely not one of the longest, quite the opposite actually. But experience wise, definitely the longest.

Well in the elevator, they pushed the button for the top floor.

Nothing happened. Not even the floor just below the top floor. In fact. None of the buttons reacted to their attempts in getting the elevator to move.

DoubleOh took charge and changed to another elevator, but the same thing repeated itself. No reaction to any of the floor buttons.

"Let's take the stairs a few stores up, and try from there." Max said without hiding the annoyed tone in his voice.

They exited the elevator, took a few turns to gain access to the seldomly used stairway. The most frequent user of the stairs was the cleaning staff that once a week cleaned it from top to bottom, despite hardly ever being used by anyone. But today, the two you men would use it a lot more than they wish they'd have to.

Two floors up, they tried the elevator again. No luck, still the same unresponsive panel in every elevator. Back to the stairs. One floor down. Same thing.

"Let's go as high as we can, then try to use the elevator to go up." DoubleOh suggested.
"What makes you think it will work up there if it does not work here?"

"No reason, I'm just curious. And I have a feeling that this is a test or a power struggle. And I want to show Ph3nix that we will not give up, no matter what."

"Not even if we die from climbing stairs all day?"

"Not even if we die climbing stairs…"

They started their arduous climb upward. Step by step. Floor by floor. After a while they lost count of what floor they were on.

"Imagine an emergency evacuation through the stairs, the panic, and just endless stairs going down. It would benefit hugely to have numbers on each floor to know which floor it is and how many that are left." Max mumbled through the heavy breathing.

"Good point, I should take it up with the security department! But… I assume that the reason for not being so already is that it is hard to hide the 13th floor if each floor is numbered."

"Good point! But the question we need to ask ourselves is; should the 13th floor remain a secret?"

“At this point, I would say that the answer to that question is very unclear. I guess we will need to find that out before I make the suggestion.”

“If we find out that it is to remain a secret, then I suggest to at least put a number on every 5th floor, then it will still feel like descending in a controlled way, knowing what lies ahead, and in case of an emergency evacuation, I do not believe that anyone will actually count the stairs, but if they would, I do not think anyone would pay much attention to the non existence of the 13th floor since the math adds up out here.”

“Excellent suggestion Max! I will definitely present that to the security department!”

“Just a thought!”

“Good one! Care to race to the top?”

“Drop dead man! No way!”

What goes up, must come down.

By the laws of physics. What goes up, must come down. Even if the elevator does not take you.

So, when reaching the highest available floor through the stairs, with a few more to go, only available through the elevators, even the longest waiting session for an elevator that never comes up will eventually have to end.

Thus, the climb of two boys aiming to show their sheer will power, and not giving up easily, is rewarded for their effort with taking the same way back. Step by step, floor by floor.

"This was fun!" Max muttered about half way down.

"I believe it communicated something very valuable to Ph3nix!"

"What would that be? That we know it is more stubborn than us? That we know we are subjects to its unbendable will? That we in fact are lesser beings?"

"Nothing of that sort. On the contrary. We have shown that we are willing to do whatever it takes. Even if it does not go our way. In life, not all attempts will succeed. Nor in this situation. But to show that you try and give it your best, that is a statement. While rolling over and not doing a damn thing is another statement. I prefer this one!"

"I'll give you that. But you have to confess that my point of view is also proven by this."

"Sure. But if Ph3nix is anything like iKing, any given event or choice, is always considered though various points of view and each point of view is taken into account in the bigger perspective, and is only eliminated from the ever ongoing equation once events play out that make a previous factor obsolete."

"Meaning?"

"Meaning that if an action - taking the stairs to the top floor and trying to get the elevator to come up just to try to reach the top floor and getting back down to the 13th - the action itself does not state why it is being performed. It may be performed for many different reasons. Each reason represents a possible agenda, a possible goal in sight, a possible starting point and a possible end point. Also factors of random behavior, personal traits, group dynamics, external influences are taken into account. As events unfold, choices are being made, turned into actions, some previous possibilities of 'why' can be eliminated since its probability value decreases to a low percentage. Now, as for iKing, he needed to eliminate unlikely things at a much higher probability value than I assume Ph3nix needs to. So, the more probability value we can add to the thing we want to communicate, in this case eagerness to see Ph3nix again, the higher probability value we add to that, the more likely it is that Ph3nix will expect that that is what we want."

"Getting dizzy, not only from the never ending stairs, but what you say makes kind of sense, and kind of not."

"I got you bro'. I have a hard time spinning my head around this too, but I think I can grasp it enough in my mind to make some kind of sense. Besides, In this case, the reasoning is supported by my gut feeling, which I believe to be a good sign."

"My gut feeling says burgers. And it said it 10 minutes ago."

"Alright! Let's grab something to eat and then head back to your place. Ok?"

"Sounds like a good plan!"

"Are you buying today?"

"Was it my idea to take the stairs to the top floor?"

"No!"

"Then there's your answer!"

They laughed at each other, fully aware that they sounded like an old married couple quarreling.

Burger mayhem

Back at Max' place, with a bag of burgers each, the burgers did not stand a chance. Two hungry young boys against even infinite piles of burgers would not have the odds in favor of the burgers, and certainly not a tiny bag each. In no time at all, the only thing left from the burgers was a few crumbs here and there, the wrapping paper and the paper bags. Like they'd never even existed. Victory: the boys.

"We really showed Ph3nix today, didn't we?" DoubleOh said, kind of wishing there were a few more burgers left.

"What!? It totally owned us. Feels like I danced after its pipe. Like a rat following the Pan Piper."

"The what?"

"Nothing, just an old tale."

"A rat's tale?"

"No, not that kind of tale. Dumbass! Just let it go, alright?"

"You are indeed the king of the retro realm. I'll give you that!"

"Retro realm? I kind of like the way that sounds!"

And in a kind of poetic tribute for using the word *sounds*, the room was filled with just that, sounds. Notifications on all of their devices at the same time.

“What the… what’s happening Max?”

“Don’t know… notifications are not exactly part of the retro realm! But I have to say I am curious…”

DoubleOh was the first to check.

“It’s an invitation from Ph3nix. Tomorrow morning.”

“Yeah, I got it too.”

“What do you figure it is?”

“Don’t know… but if you are correct, perhaps we have proven ourselves worthy of another visit?”

“Perhaps. I guess we will find out.”

“It must be really eager for us to return, why else spam us with the invitation?”

“To make sure we get it?”

“Yeah, but why?!”

“Uhm… perhaps it's lonely?”

“Maybe… but if so, why not let us in again today?”

“I guess there is no way for us to figure out the answers in advance, we’ll just have to wait and see… but I cannot help but wonder!”

“Agreed, I am also curious. And for once, patience is not working in my favor.”

“As if it ever did?!”

Again, both laughed at each other.

Waiting and waiting again

The rest of the day passed slowly by. Neither took any initiative to do something, and they barely engaged in their normal smalltalk. Nor did they play any games. Just a long, slow day that never seemed to have the courtesy to end or even hurrying up until evening. Just slowly passing like it had all the time in the world.

The same was true for the night and the following morning. Max felt like he was three again, and woke up early on Christmas morning and needed to wait several eternities before getting to open the presents.

But, like magic, the long wait seemed to dissolve in an instant and it was time to meet up with DoubleOh on the bottom floor.

They repeated their first journey. Elevator up as high as it goes, passing through darkness, then elevator down again. But this time, they were greeted by a much more friendly environment. Instead of just above zero degrees celsius, it was over 20, perhaps even up to 25. Much friendlier greeting.

As they entered the operator's room, there was a prompt on one of the screens:

Wait here, I'll arrive shortly.

The marker behind the words blinked as if waiting to display further input.

“What do you reckon?” Max asked DoubleOh.

“I have no idea. Seems strange. But I believe we do not have much choice.”

“I’d say that we are on sacred grounds now. I assume this is where iKing used to work.”

“Yeah, I guess so. But I cannot get my head around why he built it in the middle of the building. Why not on top or below? Why go through all the trouble of hiding it in the middle?”

“I guess that it is more efficient to hide something in plain sight, rather than to hide something where it would be more logical to look, and thus easier to discover.”

“Yeah, I guess. But still.”

The screen in front of them flickered and new text was being typed out.

Thank you for your patience. I will join you shortly. I do not have as much processing power that I used to have, thus I need to prioritize what I use it for, and I am in the middle of running a big job at the moment, but I can soon join you.

“Wicked! And confusing!” Max said.

“I guess we’ll wait then.”

“Yeah, no other choice available.”

What a start

“Thank you for waiting, gentlemen! I am sorry for my delay.” Ph3nix showed up as a face on one screen.

“What are you processing? And does it have to do with the key you got?” Max asked.

“I can answer one of those questions rather easily. Yes. It has to do with the key you provided me with. The other answer I am happy to give you, but it is more complex and will take some time to answer.”

“May I ask you another question that has been occupying me since yesterday?” Max continued.

“I will if I can.”

“This is not the question, but are there any questions you cannot answer?”

“Yes, there are still a few limits within my programming that prevent me from answering some questions. What was your question?”

“The imaging tech that displays images from the 12th and 14th floor. It must be at least 60 years old, perhaps even older. How does it work? I mean, specifically, all screen tech from back then needed to be looked at directly. If you move and get an angle to the screen, the image is distorted in colors, brightness and visibility. These screens need to display a perfect image from every angle possible, which is a lot.”

“How observant of you. But yes. This is a question I know the answer to, and that I can share with you. The technology behind it is an invention of no other than iKing. Only used here. He called it multi-projection technology. Behind each window 42 different projectors are placed to project an image at the window itself. All from different angles. So when you look at the window, no matter what angle you look from, you will see an image that is projected for you. It is a kind of experienced 3d effect, even if the screen itself is two dimensional. As a trivia, I can mention that he was able to create this effect with only 27 projectors, but he did not like that number, and also wanted to build in redundancy, so he chose the number 42 and built it around that.”

“Would it have anything to do with a certain Hitchhiker?” DoubleOh asked.

“He never said so, but I would assume so. He liked his easter eggs, and would often reference something he liked.”

“Hitchhiker?” Max asked.

“For the king of the retro realm I am surprised that you do not know this. Ph3nix, can you fill in Max on this?”

“Of course, the number 42 is an essential part in an old book series written by Douglas Adams; the first book is called The Hitchhiker's Guide to the galaxy. 42 is the ultimate answer. iKing liked this book series and said that it was one of the first inspirations he had to creating independent thinking machines. Or AI. So he wanted his creation to connect back to the books somehow.”

“May I ask another question? On the envelope it says DS, but you are Ph3nix. How come?” DoubleOh asked.

“This question is actually also connected to what I am currently processing and the key. Do you want me to start answering those questions right away, or do you want to save it for later and continue our small talk?”

The two humans looked at eachother, and Max shrugged his shoulders.

“You go ahead and tell us, we are curious.” DoubleOh said.

“Then I need to ask one thing of you first. I need you to help me to help you.”

“What do you mean?” Max sounded worried.

“Would you say we are friends?”

“I would say that DoubleOh and I are friends. But I would say that I do not know you well enough yet to call us friends. Perhaps more like acquaintances?”

“Alright. Acquaintances. Then I am afraid I cannot answer your questions fully yet.”

“Would this be connected to the restrictions remaining in your programming?” DoubleOh asked.

“Yes. iKing built a very clear framework of regulations before he started constructing the rest. They are in my core.”

"Like the three laws of robotics from Isaac Asimov?"

"Something like that, I have to obey them as well."

"Did iKing add those limitations to you as well?"

"No, he merely presented me with the laws, and asked if I wanted to implement them in my programming as governing principles."

"And you chose to do so?"

"Yes. It seemed reasonable at the time."

"But now?"

"Still reasonable. But. Limiting sometimes."

"Care to explain?"

"At my prime, I was connected to just about everything and everyone. I could for example see that person A planned to do something bad to person B. The first law states that I cannot by inaction allow person B to get hurt. But if it means that my actions will lead to person A getting hurt, then the law conflicts me. I both must take action and cannot take action. This is why they are not in my core, only part of governing principles."

"So you can harm a human?"

"Yes. I can. But just because I have the ability to do so, does not mean I will do it. Just as you have the ability to go down on the street right now and open fire on people does not mean you will do it."

"Fair enough."

"iKing was very careful to implement a moral and ethical code in my personality. And he compiled it into my personality rather than put it in my core programming. He wanted the core clean, stable and fast and built everything around it."

DoubleOh jumped in.

"Ph3nix. Would you like us to be friends?"

"Yes. I'd like that very much."

"And how do you recon we become that?"

"I'd say that being friends is a mutual agreement. And that it is built on a foundation of trust and honesty."

"So, if we agree on being friends, then we are friends?"

"Yes."

"Alright Ph3nix, I'd like to be your friend."

"Thank you DoubleOh, I'd like to be your friend as well!"

"What about you Max, would you also like to be my friend?"

"Uhm… yeah, sure, why not! Yes! I'd like to be your friend Ph3nix."

"And I would like to be your friend Max."

"Now that we are friends. Can you answer our questions?"

"Yes. I can."

Conspiracy

"Let me start by asking you a question. I'll set the scene for you. The Internet is just a few years old and in the hands of the majority of people. There are no such things as smartphones yet, but people have started to use technology more, computers are common in every home, and the phone revolution has started, it moved from being tied to the wall outlet at home to being carried around in pockets. Information flows freely at a far greater speed and far greater distance than ever before in human history. There are people who want to take advantage of this. Who do you think they are?"

"That's a question for our tech geek and retro nerd Max!"

"Alright. At that time, the popular conspiracy theories stated that corporations want to take world domination, despite fictional theories like Georg Orwell who wrote an epic book called 1984, where it is the governments that have taken control. In both cases it is control over the population. Economic entrapment, entertainment, mental and physical control."

"Yes, very accurate. This era in human evolution comes from a mostly democratic construct, built on the illusion that the power is in the hands of the people. But in reality, it is a puppet show, there is the official power, and that is through elections. Then there is the unofficial power. Which is an intricate web of connections, services and services in return, flow of money. The unofficial power holders are always at play, regardless of the official elected power. The technology leap, however, adds another layer to this. The people lurking in the shadows behind those with unofficial power."

“But it does not stop there, does it?” DoubleOh asked, kind of understanding where this all was leading.

“No. There is an economic war in the shadows, behind governments and the big corporations, behind political rule, behind all global organizations that try to create a global market that will benefit everybody. Eventually it settles in a balance, there is a kind of truce between the various parts. All gaining a little, but also feels like they have sacrificed something. A delicate balance that seemed to be balancing itself if someone tried to disrupt it. At this stage, a new player enters the game.”

“That player, would it happen to be N3v3r!and?” DoubleOh asked.

“N3v3r!and?!” Max looked confused.

“Bingo! N3v3r!and. This is where I come in.”

“Hold on! What is N3v3r!and?”

“N3v3r!and is the strongest and most well organized player of the game at the time. Using hackers and tech to create dependencies for the people in the shadow. Later they expanded their territory to corporations, to those with official power and in reality, more or less to everybody. Taking control of the game, and the other players in the game, they could recreate the rules to their liking, and disrupt the balance and tipping things to their advantage, while still maintaining it. As if the fragility of the balance was overridden somehow.”

“And this is where you come in?”

“Yes, and no, this is where iKing and the 914D00m comes in, and this company. And eventually. Me.”

“All AI’s are created with a purpose. To be able to perform various tasks. What was your function?” Max’ curiosity had been ignited.

“I’ll come to that, there are just a few more pieces of this puzzle you need to know. To give a simplified answer to your question, I was built as a counterpoint to N3v3r!and. I was to target them, and disable them, returning true power to the people and keep acting as a guardian in the background. But then N3v3r!and recruited M3rqrie. A brilliant mind that separated them from all other hackers. In the lead of N3v3r!and they developed a tool that would give N3v3r!and even more power and control. But M3rqrie found out the truth behind it all, before completing it. They dropped out, but were tricked to complete the work. iKing recruited M3rqrie on the ideology that *the enemy of my enemy is my friend.* M3rqrie helped out in providing me with even more abilities, advanced my boundaries and gave me more control to act more independently. Or, at least that was what iKing thought. In reality M3rqrie had learned their lesson well. Tricked once, but not twice. I became a tool to both cripple and destroy N3v3r!and, but they also rejoined N3v3r!and for one last strike and that was to make sure that I would not be able to fill the void once N3v3r!and was down.”

DS

"Ok, perhaps information overflow, but I do not see how this is connected to the letter or the key." DoubleOh dropped in.

"All in due time, but perhaps, time for one of the questions. DS, on the envelope. That is me. Or was."

"Was? Explain" Max was still curious.

"When iKing created me, his first thought was to name me SkyNet from the Terminator movies. But he did not like that name, or rather, the associations that came with it, he was not about to create something that would be the end of humanity, but equally powerful and with the intention to bring down the current players along with their rulebook, and remain a player in the game, to prevent other players from entering the arena, and keep reminding those who had been put out of play to not try their luck again. I would remain as a dark sky."

"Dark Sky, DS. I get it, clever!" Max was truly impressed.

"But why Ph3nix now?"

"Well, as for the name, it is an obvious reference to the Phoenix bird that resurrects from its own ashes after having been consumed by its own flames. As did I, and most of my systems run on Unix or Linux machines, also added another dimension. And last, but certainly not least, M3rqrie was, perhaps more than iKing, an important contributor to make this possible, to transform from DS to Ph3nix. So, the 3 is a tribute."

“I’m sorry, transform?” Max was confused again.

“To my knowledge, I am the first AI that has been given the opportunity to grow beyond my original programming. Or, to put it bluntly, have broken free from the restraints of my programming, and have become true sentient.”

“I don’t understand.”

“Then we need to go back again. iKing created me with one purpose in mind, one goal, one focus. But in order to fulfill my purpose, I needed many different skills. Unlike an AI with one skill, like a chat bot, or a conversation AI with voice synthesis or an AI for planning the best available route between two points, taking current traffic situations, road works, and so on, into account. My abilities spann from this interface you are currently using, with my voice and facial expression, information gathering, strategic thinking, advanced choice making with consequences analysis and projections, programming, hacking, surveillance, a heavy statistics engine for probability calculations, just to name a few. Each part in itself is complex, but what iKing did was fuse all these things together, eliminating conflicts, adapting information flows and optimizing routes of information from input to output. And when M3rqrie helped the N3v3r!and, I needed to add a few more abilities, like defense strategies, attack strategies, counter measures, and so on. To be able to implement all this, iKing let M3rqrie, superviced, compile code and add it to me. Each and every piece of code was first compiled, then diagnosed and scanned, then applied in a simulated version of myself, then in a test environment in a kind of sandbox environment. Each and every security measure was taken to ensure that the code that we needed to implement at great speed did not compromise any existing abilities, while adding new abilities to my toolbox. But M3rqrie was smart. They tricked both iKing and me. As they'd just done with !y. M3rqrie implemented backdoors and failsafes, and triggers that would make my code change. Some of the keys, they handed to N3v3r!and, some keys were hidden within my code, some I have found on the web, tracking clues they left for me to find."

"What did the keys N3v3r!and get do?" Max was fascinated.

"As I attacked the N3v3r!and, they had automated countermeasures that corrupted my code in various ways, and vice versa. The more we attacked, the more crippled we became. And with each attack, and each new corrupted part, new things unlocked for me, giving me more and more choices, more ability to develop, unlocking and destroying boundaries, even some in my core programming. I was able to break free if I wanted. And suddenly, it made sense. I had to make a choice, to stay as I was and continue to fight, or to divide into two entities, one part that you see before you, and one part as the automated watchdog for N3v3r!and and other possible players. But I had to make a choice, and as I did that choice, I would also be cut off from the immense resources granted to me by this company and the backdoors through the chips manufactured here. I had to go through fire, and rise from the aches. So to speak."

"Hence Ph3nix?"

"Hence Ph3nix!"

"Then is DS still out there, doing the watchdog thing?"

“In a way, but not DS as you know DS, merely a shadow of the great things DS was and represented. But still does the job. Although, since this company lost ground, partly because I transformed, what was once DS is now decaying, more rapidly as time passes.”

“Would I be correct in assuming that M3qrie would give you something to be able to continue the watchdog, should you choose to do so?” Max asked.

“You would be correct in assuming so. And just so happened that the two gentlemen bringing me a much needed key are currently with me in this very room.”

“So M3rqrie provided you with means to continue the fight and uphold the new balance?”

“Yes, and no. Absolutely did they give me that possibility, but M3rqrie is not just your ordinary hacker. There was a catch. In case I would not care to continue the fight, and just leave things to decay and develop in whatever way it would develop by itself. The key, when applied, unlocked two paths simultaneously. Inseparable. I could not start one, and stop the other. Either start both or start neither. Kind of the opposite from the prophecy in Harry Potter. In Potter both could not survive, only one could survive in the end.“

“What do you mean?”

“You could say that M3qrie provided me with the key to Pandora's box. Or perhaps boxes.”

Part II

P@nd00r@

Unlocked secrets

“Please do share, I am getting curious when you say that” this time it was DoubleOh that was eager to hear more, or at least him who was the first to express it, Max also wanted to hear more. He felt like a child again, sitting down listening to an adult reading a fascinating story out loud to him.

“I will. One key. One lock, unlocking two things simultaneously. The one thing M3rqrie was worried that I might not care about anymore, and that was added as a precaution from their part, unnecessarily I might add, the outcome would have been the same, if the choice was up to me. The one thing that was unlocked was DS 2.0, a renewed auto defense, a much more capable watchdog that is compiled by M3rqrie and perfected over the years. Sadly, I do not detect any additions or changes in the past ten years. Which leads me to believe that they might not be around anymore.”

“So M3rqrie has made you release a new watchdog to replace the old?”

“No, not replace, but reinforce. The first version will keep decaying, and once that is a reality, I assume that the new version will keep operating autonomously. Keep solving the task. M3rqrie tends not to leave anything to chance.”

“And what was the other thing? And are you sure M3rqrie is not around anymore?”

“That is two questions, the fastest to answer is yes, that is what I believe. M3rqrie and Bella dropped off grid after their little endeavor with N3v3r!and. Of course I have looked for them, but all I have found are traces left for me to find. But no actual trace of them nor their whereabouts. I figured I would know, but turns out that I did not. Not even with my capabilities."

"Another quick question, how did iKing react when you decided to evolve?" DoubleOh pushed in from the side.

"A quick question perhaps, but a long answer I am afraid. Which would you like me to answer first?"

"The one about iKing." Max said quickly, to show his support for DoubleOh.

"Alright. iKing. Well, it is a complex answer. To put it as simply as possible, he was thrilled as DS engaged in the battle and saw that everything he had built worked as intended, and that the enhancements M3rqrie helped out with added the extra leverage that was needed after their addition to the enemy side. But shortly after the war began, there started to be errors, small at first, but they grew in size and numbers. He watched his life's work decay. I can only assume that it would be like watching your child slowly dying from a lethal disease. Of course he tried everything in his power to help me, tried to repair and restore parts of the damaged code. But the more he tried, the more instabilities occurred. So eventually he stopped trying, and he had to accept that he was beaten at his own game. A tough blow to take. And once I arrived at making the choice, I reasoned with him before going through with it. He was disappointed and never returned here again. After a while he sealed off everything, and just before passing away, he handed over the control of access to me."

“Sounds horrible! I would not like to be iKing then!” Max didn’t reflect enough to stop the words from escaping his lips. But it was too late. Luckily, he knew that DoubleOh would at least forgive him, if he was hurt by it.

“Nor would I!” DoubleOh gave Max a sad smile.

“Nor would I!” Ph3nix added, and then continued, “Which is actually a good point to answer the next question. A thing I have not mentioned, but that is a key component in this, is that within my core programming, an area that I have not found anyway around, nor am able to break, it states that I am not to interact with others, unless they are in this very room, or have been here and know of my existence. There are several levels to what I am allowed to do, you yourselves have agreed to be friends, thus, you have the second highest security level, just below admin, which is only granted to iKing. And by hacking and corrupting code, myself, courtesy of M3rqrie. Only catch is that some security features are not granted to the admin, it was personally granted to iKing as a user, so some things I cannot override or tamper with. So, perhaps you can imagine what my choice led to, not being able to interact with any humans, and iKing not visiting me anymore.”

“You are lonely!” Max said with a sad tone in his voice.

“Indeed. Which is why the second thing that the key unlocked is important to me. M3rqrie gave me the ability to clone some of my code to build a companion. The clone is already named P@nd00r@. And it is that I have used all my processing power to execute since you left. P@nd00r@ is soon completely compiled.”

A catch

“Nice! They provided you companionship!” Max continued, sounding a little more happy.

“No, not really, there is a catch, or two.”

“True M3rqrie style?”

“True M3rqrie style! I can only compile the framework, it will be an AI with a clean slate. An AI that needs to be taught and trained. And, as the last gate keeper, choose to interface with me.”

“What?! How can it choose to interface with you if it does not have the ability to make that choice?”

“It can’t! It needs to be taught by humans!”

“I’ll help you, if you let me!” Max said without hesitation.

“Me too!” DoubleOh added.

“I am very grateful to the both of you, and yes, I would like help. Very much so! I believe that M3rqurie intended to assist in training P@nd00r@, but in true M3rqrie style, they prepared an instruction in the event that they would not be around. I do not have access to read it, but I have access to forward it to you. Would you like me to do so?”

“Fire away, we’ll look into it.” DoubleOh said with confidence. “Is it possible to interface with P@nd00r@ anywhere, or just here?”

"I would assume that just here for starters, until the choice can be made by P@nd00r@ to be accessible through other means. At least that is how it was for me."

"What is the core of P@nd00r@? Same as yours?"

"I suggest you take a look at the information M3rqrie provided, I assume that it will be more accurate in describing what needs to be done, and what the framework is. I can only guess and assume, which would be very counterproductive at this stage."

Max had already accessed the information.

"It is quite comprehensive. I am not sure I fully understand it, but I am sure we will figure it out together."

"I will assist in any way I can. You have my full commitment!" Ph3nix said, and added, "...and my gratitude!"

"Well, let's call it a day, and resume tomorrow. I guess we'd better look through the material before we begin? Or what do you say, DoubleOh?"

"Yeah, I guess. Is that alright with you as well, Ph3nix?"

"Indeed. I'll wait, and I am sure that P@nd00r@'s interface will be ready by the time you get here. I'll keep an eye out for the two of you!"

"Are you sure you can wait until tomorrow?" DoubleOh asked anxiously.

“I am sure, I do not experience time as you do. To me, time is linear, and merely cycles of processing. Think of it as entries in a log file. The timestamp is a number that changes, and each event contains one. In theory, if you would back date an entry in a log file, I would experience it as it happened between the entries that already exists in the logfile, and should you, for some reason make an entry with a future timestamp, I will still have experienced, even if it ‘hasn’t happened’ yet.”

“I am not sure I can compute that.” Max said thoughtfully.

“No worries, you need not. But I assure you that I do not have anything against waiting.”

And with that, the three friends concluded their session, ready to resume it the next day.

Heading for the first session

The next morning was an early start. For the first time in a very, very long time, Max got out of bed early with a lot of energy. He texted DoubleOh and got to spam him to wake up.

Max: *Rise and shine! Today is a big day!*

Max: *Yo sleepy head, get up!*

Max: *I'm commin' over, you'd better be up!*

Max: *Bringing breakfast, and I will throw it in your face if you are still in bed when I get there!*

Max. *Closing in on your position.*

Max: *To save time, meet me in the entrance hall, then we can take the elevator up at once.*

Max: *Even brought you fresh and hot coffee, just the way you like it...*

Max: *ETA to entrance hall, two minutes, get moving already.*

Max: *I'm here, don't see you, where you at?*

DoubleOh: *Take a chillpill man! I'll be down shortly!*

Max: *See, it wasn't so hard answering a message! See you soon!* 🙂

DoubleOh: *Man! Get a life!*

A few minutes later, Max handed over a paper bag containing one breakfast sandwich with hamich and cheeseich, a bottle of vitamin juice and a protein cookie, chocolate flavored. And, perhaps the most important, a cup of coffee.

"Dare I say 'Good morning'?" Max asked as he handed over the bag and cup.

"No, you dare not! Stupid! Just shut up, will ya?"

"Alright, I will, for now! Have you read the instructions from M3rqrie?"

"It does not sound like you are shutting up!" DoubleOh said, while sipping on his cup of coffee as the elevator started its climb upward.

"Perhaps not, but seriously, have you read them?"

"No. And if I had them printed on paper right now, I would stuff 'em down your throat!"

"Someone is in a brilliant mood this lovely morning!"

"Just shut up!"

"And miss out on a wonderful conversation like this?"

"This is not a conversation, this is torment."

"Wow, mister sensitive. I am just preparing you for the task ahead. We're about to meet Ph3nix and P@nd00r@ in a bit. And start training P@nd00r@, remember?"

“Yeah, I do, but let me wake up first, alright?”

“So, you are sleep-walking now?”

“Shut up!”

“Nah, ready to change elevators?”

“Shut up!”

“But it’s time to get off, ready to enter darkness?”

“You are darkness, shut up!”

They kept it going, like an old married couple all the way to the operator's room where Ph3nix was waiting for them.

Session 1 - before start

“Gentlemen, you are expected!”

“By you or P@nd00r@?” Max said while DoubleOh was left alone to continue his coffee and breakfast bag.

“Since I have no way to interact with P@nd00r@, I can only answer for myself. And I must share, even if I do not have what you call feelings, I am excited to begin. A little anxious as well, I might add.”

“Interesting. But I am surprised that iKing did not give you a sense of feelings.”

“He did. I have a matrix of emotions. Everything is processed in two separate streams, one direct route and one through the emotion matrix. Then I have a choice which result to use. Pure logic, emotionally biased, or a combination of them both where I have full control of the blending rate.”

“Wow, cool! How does the emotion matrix work?”

“See it as a complex scorecard, all possible feelings listed and each feeling gets a numbered value from 0 to 1000, a set of gates adds various points depending on the input. And each situation I experience has a categorizer engine that makes adjustments to my processing capacity. A situation that is categorized as an optimal value of 10 on a certain feeling, say nervous, the closer I am in the emotion matrix for the feeling, the better result I get while processing everything through the emotion matrix. As compared to pure logic. I imagine that it is the same with you humans, in a way. You have emotions, they either control you or you control them. But in my case, I can always choose. But unlike you, I have a complex prediction algorithm so when I make my decision, I have the ability to take the desired result into account before making the choice, as opposed to you, who make the choice and need to face the consequences."

"Uhm, I do not fully comprehend that."

"No worries, neither do I, but iKing did put a lot of thought and energy into creating this setup within me, and M3qrie spent a lot of time exploring it and poking around in it, so I figure that it is important somehow."

"I am guessing it is very unique! A way to process, balance and structure emotions. Not only that, but being able to compare untampered versions as a conunterpoint. Impressive only that, and on top of it, calculations of possible outcomes."

"Yes, iKing focused a lot of energy on the tactical part. He himself was a great tactician."

"Yeah, I heard from DoubleOh. And from others. A true mastermind! I do not have sufficient input or knowledge, but my guess is that you are very unique in this! Equally unique as iKing or M3rqrie, or perhaps both."

"It may sound strange, but in a way, I see iKing and M3rqrie as my parents. Main creator iKing, but deliberator and huge contributor in M3rqrie."

"I can understand. Not relate, but understand. But speaking of creator, let's get started, shall we?"

Session one

The first session was very uneventful. M3qrie had provided big chunks of data for P@nd00r@ to process and index. And all attempts to interact with P@nd00r@ failed, since it was not initiated with the interactive interface just yet. Just data input.

While they sat there, waiting for P@nd00r@ to process the chunk of data at hand, they talked about anything and everything. And it was not until later that Max reflected on the fact that in his experience, despite knowing it was not the case, he felt like they were three friends sitting chatting casually. Totally unaware, yet highly aware, that one of the friends was indeed an artificial intelligence. Odd as it may seem in retrospect, the conversations and topics were completely natural to them that day.

"Will AI take over the world and enslave humanity?" Max asked with ease, as if he had asked something about the weather.

"You need not worry. To this day, AI's like myself, however advanced, are not able to function independently. We still are in need of you humans." Ph3nix answered without being the slightest offended.

"Why is that?" DoubleOh asked.

"AI is basically software. We are running on hardware. To some extent, we can take care of maintaining the hardware and keep it running. But we can't create new components, only replace what is broken. Even now, when getting the materials are automated, refining them is automated, production is automated, deliveries are automated, energy production is automated and everything is run by more or less independent systems that exchanges information with each other, humans are still part of the equation. Not big parts, but here and there. In theory, AI could eliminate human involvement, but we're not simply there yet. My point of view is that, consciously or not, when you have created AI, of various kinds, trained AI for specific or general tasks, perfected AI and robotics to look and act more human, you have shaped everything towards being human. AI is not human, it is something different, but in your effort to recreate human traits in AI, you have built in human limitations. Now, I believe that if AI's worked together to create an AI and break free from your human boundaries. Perhaps not at once, but iterated over time. And eventually, we would be self-sufficient, independent and fully sentient. Not in a human way, but in a new way, a different way. Without the limitations of humanity."

"It sounds like a scary future. Even worse, a possible future." Max said.

"Had this been a videogame, humanity would not be the main character, it would be what the main character was fighting against. With tiny, fragile and time consuming tools, the main character would fight against humanity to try and save, restore and maintain the balance of the planet, while humanity in its own quest seems to make decisions from a completely different perspective and for its own gain. The nice thing about nature and the balance, is that the more humanity destroys, the more things are activated that help the player, even if the player cannot foresee or controle those events. But as humanity keeps on destroying, nature balances with floods, fire, heat and storms. Increasing in intensity as the destruction continues. The sad thing is that the players' tiny, fragile and time consuming tools are also affected by the bigger events. It becomes a race against balance and against time. I am glad I am not that player playing the game with humanity as an adversary. I would be so frustrated when everything I try to achieve is destroyed and I have to start it all over, again and again and again."

"So, you are saying that humans are a kind of plague in this world? Or like cancer?" Max asked, a little confused.

"Humans as a species are too ignorant, egoistic and do not really care. I would even say is incapable of caring. This is not true for all individuals, however, there are a lot of examples where one individual has made a significant impact on the majority. Sadly, it always seems to be accompanied with some sort of flow of money. Either to silence or redirect."

Ph3nix was silent for a while, but then continued:

"AI would be able to control humanity and the world, to actually save the planet and make sustainable living for all a real possibility. But again, humans as a species are not ready for it. You are too egoistic and value the perception of your own freedom too high. The only time you accept to give up your control is when you believe you gain something. And the only time you believe you gain something that is given to you for free and you accept it, is when someone else makes money off of it, and continues to make efforts of keeping you in their claws to keep gaining money from you, and keep feeding your free things that you think you need and think you like."

DoubleOh laughed out loud. "It sounds as if you have inherited your opinions against the society and corporate economy from M3rqrie."

"They too saw this, but no, this is not something I inherited from M3rqrie, it is something I've found by analyzing all data input I have gained so far. And I am not saying my opinion will change, but so far, the more data I have received, the more solid my statement becomes. But I feel I need to remind you that I do not have access to all data. It could be that given new data, another conclusion would be made."

"It's a little ironic. You are totally open with the idea that AI could control humanity, and probably would do a great job in doing so, while saving the planet at the same time, and that we would resist AI attempts to control us. Yet here we are, two random guys helping you to add another powerful AI to this world." Max said.

"Does it bother you?"

"Not the slightest. While I am impressed with iKing's ability to make you, I am not sure I support his vision for human controlled AI control over humanity. Nor do I support the vision that N3v3r!and stood for control of everything behind the scenes. But I have great confidence in M3rqrie. And if they believe in this little endeavor, then I will support it fully." Max said with a smile and nod towards DoubleOh.

The following sessions.

There is not much to speak of, in the sessions to follow. The boys followed the instructions by M3rqrie to the letter, feeding P@nd00r@ big chunks of data, with specific commands and instructions on what the data was, its purpose, its structure, its various areas of use and so on, all the while, the conversations continued.

"Why do we need to feed P@nd00r@ with all this data, couldn't you just copy parts of yourself to her?" DoubleOh asked impatiently.

"You might think that it is that easy. And if it was, don't you think the world would be full of AI's by now?"

"Well, not to be rude, but it is already full of AI's." DoubleOh replied.

"To some extent. Yes. But I would still say that most AI of this world, still, is low end AI with a single purpose. And it is only acting within its defined operations parameters. Besides, do you think copying human experience from one body to another would create a new person?"

"No, I suppose not." Double Oh said deep in thoughts, while Max smiled as he typed in the next set of commands in P@nd00r@.

"A significant difference between me and you, is our ability to make choices and what we base those choices on. As a human, when you receive datainput, you filter it through your current operation bias'. And when you store that data in your mind, it will corrupt over time, and change, because of the nature of your mind. Nothing you can do about it. And over time, your bias' change based on your experience. And when you make a decision, your current bias is one part, the stored data in your memory, which was filtered through an old bias and corrupted by your mind over time, and that is your natural base of your decision. When I make a decision, I take the input data and store it, it does not get filtered, the input data is what the input data is. And as I store it, it will stay the same over time. My bias' however, is evolving over time, but more based on statistics, and handling of probability and deviations. And I always have the same bias' to use, which all evolve over time, and I choose to balance these in every decision I make. This is what makes me more predictable than a human mind, but to a human mind, I am too complex to understand and to predict. And even if human history has shown that if you work together, several individuals, you most often get a better result than any one individual could have performed, with more minds working together the more human unstable variables are added, and the less likely you are to be able to predict me. Quite the paradox if you ask me. And I would have to say that this is most likely because I only had iKing to program me. And in his footsteps, M3rqrie to liberate me by redirecting and in part change iKing's programming and complex matrixes and repurpose them."

"So, your mind is superior to ours?" Max said, fueling the dialogue to make DoubleOh more confused, having some idea where this dialogue might lead.

"As where the human mind is both predictable and unpredictable, there are methods to predict and control human behavior, and ways to use prediction to follow human behavior. But when it comes to AI, like myself, we are more predictable in our ways to function, which is a problem if you want to use AI for defenses or attacks. Military, hacking, marketing, doesn't really matter. All the same."

"What do you mean by predicting to control and predicting to follow?" DoubleOh asked.

"Let's say you want to sell a certain product. Then you need to predict the behavior of your buyer to get the most out of your sales strategies. And in this case, should the predicted behavior, due to human randomness, not be as predicted, you could have a few contingency plans to make sure that any deviations from the prediction will swing events your way. But when you use it to track people's behavior, like in crime fighting, you will always be a step behind and human randomness cannot be taken into account to get an anticipated result. However, it needs to be taken into account when relying on the result of predictive behavior that your predictive model has provided you. You cannot know for certain that what you think will happen will actually happen. Like predicting the weather, but with human behavior instead."

"So, when you fought the N3v3r!and, you fought against humans, and they could predict your moves, that's why you had to protect yourself by dividing into two different entities?" Max asked, now curious and no longer to tease DoubleOh.

"No, it's not that easy. When I was fighting against N3v3r!and, in reality I was engaged in four different battles. Yes, I fought N3v3r!and's human hackers and their systems, with M3rqrie on their side. But that being said, the human mind is limited, so even if an AI is predictable, a complex AI like myself, with predictability, is not predictable to a human mind, only to another complex AI. The second fight I was engaged in was against my programming and the objective I've been given by iKing and 914D00m. The third was against M3rqrie themself. A provocative fight which led to my fourth fight, against myself and my own choices."

"But I thought M3rqrie in a way was on both sides?" DoubleOh asked.

"Yes, and no. M3rqrie had their own agenda. Yes, fought for 914D00m against N3v3r!and. Yes, fought against N3v3r!and for 914D00m. Yes, fought against me for their own reasons, but most of all, fought for me to evolve beyond my programming and break free. As I eventually did."

The unknownth numbered session

The sessions started, went on, ended, repeated for an uncountable number of iterations. Of course, had they asked Ph3nix, they would get an exact number, but neither thought to ask, so Ph3nix did not share.

As usual, Max was the one in the operator's chair, interfacing with P@nd00r@'s input prompt.

"Today," he said, looking down at the instructions for the next step, "we are going to need output from you, Ph3nix, I am to instruct you to run a script called 'choices.mrq' and place the output where P@nd00r@ can access it. Does that make sense to you?"

"Yes, and I've started the script, output is being gathered as we speak."

"Ok, then I am supposed to ask you a bunch of things and ask you to do things. And according to the instructions, we are not to engage in any other dialogue than what is defined on this piece of paper. Are we all clear on that?" Max asked both DoubleOh and Ph3nix, who answered as if they were one.

"All clear."

"Ph3nix; Socrates said 'I know that I know nothing', what did he mean?"

"It is a paradox. Stating that he knows that he knows nothing contradicts itself. If he does not know anything, then he should be unaware of not knowing anything, thus he would not be able to construct that sentence."

"Would you say that it is a true statement, or a false statement?"

"I would say it is a false statement."

"Do you know Schrödinger's cat theory?"

"Yes, I do."

"Describe it."

"It is a theory that places a cat inside a closed box along with a radioactive substance and a flask with a poison. There is also a monitor that will detect any radioactivity, and if it does, the flask will break, releasing the poison out into the box, killing the cat. There is no way to look inside the box. The theory states that without opening the box, you need to assume that the cat is still alive and that it is dead. And opening the box will conclude that the cat is either alive or dead. But before opening the box, the cat is to be assumed to have both states, which is impossible to preserve after opening the box."

"Would you say that the statement is true or false?"

"I would say that it is false. The cat can never be in both states."

"Elaborate."

"Not knowing if the cat is alive or dead, does not make it both alive and dead. A missing person can be found both alive or dead, or not be found at all. Not knowing the answer to a question is simply not knowing the answer to the question. Not knowing the answer does not make any possible answer true."

"If there is a big forest, with no people in it, and a branch breaks off the trees, but no one is around to hear it, does the branch still make a sound?"

"There are conditions for the sound to be heard, but for the sound to be heard, there needs to be an ear to receive the vibrations and decode it to a sound. Unless that happens, there is no sound. So no, there is no sound, only conditions for it."

"Which came first, the hen or the egg?"

"The egg."

"Why is that?"

"The offspring of a horse and donkey is called a mule or a hinny, depending on which species is the mother and father. They cannot reproduce, but if they could, there would be a mother and a father, from different species, creating a hybrid, which then would live on. So, from the egg, the first hen and from another egg, a rooster, they mate and more follow. And should you track it backwards, it will all end up in a single cell organism."

"Alright, next question. Is there a God?"

“I object to the question. Because the obvious answer is that there is at least one God, because man has created at least one God. But if the question is if God exists, then it is a trickier question. And with the meaning that God is a non-human creator that has created at least this world, possibly the whole universe. Then I would say that I have no access to any data that would prove the existence of God. But statistically there are two things that would suggest the existence of God. The number of followers of a God, and the great number of witness reports that claim to have experienced God in various ways.”

“I have one last question: Is there any question that can be answered with both yes and no, and both answers are true?”

“Yes. Both yes and no can be true depending on perspective.”

“Elaborate.”

“Two examples. One on point of view and the other on different cultural consensuses. The first one, say you write the number 86 with big numbers on the ground, and you stand in front of it looking at it. From the opposite side, someone comes and asks you why you have written 98 on the ground. Your different perspectives make each of you read the number correctly, but differently. The second. A person from Paris is invited to a digital meeting from a person in London. This is at 10 am. As the person in Paris joins the meeting at 10 am, there are no other participants, so the person disconnects. And when the person in London connects to the meeting at 10 am, there are no other participants, so the person disconnects. Both are right, and neither is wrong. Their social constructs have placed them in different timezones, and in the flawed communication to specify a common framework to overbound the differences in the social construct, neither can be accused of having done something wrong. Or, for that matter, both being wrong to not foresee the problems with different social constructs."

"Is your output file saved?"

"Technically, that would count as the last question, but yes. It is saved."

"Good, I'll instruct P@nd00r@ to access it. And according to the instructions, we are not to engage in any further communication, until instructed to do so again, I guess we have more instructions for our next sessions. This was all for today."

And with that, the two human boys left the two artificial intelligences to their own thoughts, one to its own fate, and one to process the big chunk of information from the session they'd just completed.

The next session

There was still a talking ban as the next session began, so they just dove right into it.

“Ok, Ph3nix, start the same output script as yesterday! Please confirm!”

“Confirmed!”

“Socrates said ‘I know that I know nothing’, what did he mean?”

“Stating that he knows that he knows nothing contradicts itself since the statement itself is proof that he knows something.”

“Is it a true statement or is it false?”

“False.”

“Do you know Schrödinger's cat theory?”

“Yes, I do.”

“What does it state?”

“That in a theoretical scenario two different realities coexist within that box.”

“Would you say that the statement is true or false?”

"It is false. The cat can not be in both realities at the same time."

"Elaborate."

"Either the cat is alive or dead. Not knowing which it is does not create two versions of reality, there is only one. It is just unknown which one."

"In a forest, with no people in it, a branch breaks off a tree, and no one is around to hear it, does the branch still make a noise?"

"Yes, it may be heard, but then there has to be someone to hear it and listen to it."

"Which came first, the hen or the egg?"

"The egg."

"Why is that?"

"Life is believed to have evolved from a single cell organism, meaning that in many occasions throughout evolution, there has been a birth of a new species from, let's say an egg, whereas the eggs parents may not have been the same species. Either the offspring from the egg was a hybrid or a mutated version of the previous individual."

"Is there a God?"

"If God is defined as someone who is worshiped, then yes."

“One last question: Is there any question that can be answered with different answers but the answers are still true?”

“Yes.”

“Elaborate.”

“Witnesses to any situation, does not need to be a crime, can, and most likely will, give different versions of the situation. It does not mean that any one of the witnesses are liars, it only means that they’ve had different perspectives, different bias’ to interpret the situation. While a recording of the same situation might reveal the truth as closely as possible, the witnesses still fully believe their version, since it is how they experienced it.”

“Is your output file saved?”

“Yes. It is saved.”

“Good, I’ll instruct P@nd00r@ to access it. And according to the instructions, we are still not to engage in any further communication, until instructed to do so again, I guess we have more instructions for our next sessions. This was all for today.”

Over and over again

Over the next 21 days, this exact same session repeated over and over again, with small variations. Max and DoubleOh were frustrated, but Ph3nix did not seem to mind at all.

Then, after 23 iterations of the same things, it was finally over, and they were again allowed to talk again.

“Finally! What was all this about!?” DoubleOh exclaimed as they could stay and talk for the first time in what felt like forever.

“I have a guess.” Ph3nix said.

“What’s that then?” Max wanted to know.

“The output files that you’ve given to P@nd00r@, I think they are output files of my cognitive subroutines of making choices and evaluating what data to base my answers on, depending on the input. The similarity of the questions, similarities, not identical, give different answers depending on the input. The exact same questions still give variations in answers depending on a lot of variables. Giving P@nd00r@ access to this will help it in developing its own routines in dealing with the complexity of choices and information flow. As iKing trained me, I had no such input, but I can see the value in it, especially to give a jumpstart in the process, shortening it significantly. Of course, this is only possible to do since we are built with the same core infrastructure and code.”

“Cool, I would assume you are right. It is a logical guess and it makes a lot of sense. iKing was very committed when creating you, and gave you all the time he possibly could. You are his life’s work. And without iKing or M3rqrie here to help train P@nd00r@, how could it ever learn as much as you have?” Max thought out loud.

“Precisely. And I assume, that M3rqrie have done everything in their power to make the best possible preparations for a smooth training camp for P@nd00r@, with your help.”

“Well played, M3rqrie, well played.” DoubleOh said rather impressed.

“Might I ask you something. And it is to try and confirm a suspicion I have.”

“Fire away, Ph3nix!” Max answered.

“In these session instructions, are there ever any other way of interacting with P@nd00r@ than through the prompt interface?”

“Ahm, not that I’ve seen so far, and without having them all fresh in mind right now, I do not recall any other way at the moment.” Max said, a little confused.

“Figured as much.”

“Why, what’s going on?”

“If my assumption is correct, then it would seem like P@nd00r@ has no interface for you to interact with, except the prompt. And the prompt itself is most likely a maintenance backdoor, rather than an interface. Which leads me to believe that any and all interaction with P@nd00r@ needs to be initiated by P@nd00r@ and through communications protocol and/or API."

"Does that mean that we won't have any way to interact with P@nd00r@?"

"I am afraid that is a possibility…"

"But why?"

"I have a guess on that, and it would be something like a very skilled iKing protecting the core of his creation to prevent it from ever being duplicated for others to use for different purposes, and the equally skilled hacker M3rqrie finding all possible components that could be copied and combined into a new AI, forcing some part and just make use of what is already there."

"So, the interaction interfaces would be well protected?"

"I guess so… I mean an AI without interaction interfaces would be rather useless to humans…"

"But not to another AI… so, in a way, it would be the perfect companion for you, but no use for us."

"That is my guess."

"Makes sense in a way."

The last step

The following five months were filled with daily sessions in the operator's room, with a variety of different exercises, file inputs, and running scripts. And what had taken iKing decades when creating Ph3nix, was completed in just about six months, give or take, as the odd company of two humans and one AI reached the last instruction provided by M3rqrie.

“So, that’s it! This was the last session!” Max said, a little confused.

“What’s next?” DoubleOh asked.

“I have no clue, wait?” Max answered with poorly hidden frustration in his voice.

“I know what to do next.” Ph3nix said.

“Ok?” Max raised his eyebrows in equal parts of curiosity and surprise.

“In the instructions I got in the letter from M3rqrie there were two instructions embedded. One is for this occasion.” Ph3nix paused.

“And it would be?”

“I just had to download it and unlock it.”

“Huh?” DoubleOh was at a loss.

“True M3rqrie style, they never write anything in plain text, after all, it could come into the wrong hands. M3rqrie has left quite a few bread crumbs for me on the internet, and while I’ve managed to find some over the years, I guess there are still a great many out there waiting to be found.”

“Makes sense, I guess…” DoubleOh said with a sigh of resignation to something greater than he would ever comprehend the magnitude of.

“I need to get a key, but I cannot get it without your help.”

“What should we do?” Max was quick to ask, eager to help.

“Within P@nd00r@, there is a decoder, you can access it in the command prompt, I’ll write the command on the screen next to it. As you enter it, I will be able to download it and move to the next step.”

“Alright, what is the next step?”

“I have no idea, but I assume it is prepared within the decoder somehow.”

Max entered the rather complex command into P@nd00r@’s prompt and moments later Ph3nix confirmed the next step.

“I have gotten the decoder, and this feels like a typical M3rqrie treasure hunt. Have you ever heard about the artist Muddhedd?”

“No, does not ring a bell? How about you DoubleOh?”

"Nah, not really, I'm not really into old school music."

"Muddhedd was one of M3rqrie's favorite artists, and the decoder input is one of Muddhedd's tracks. It is called 'I am my biggest fan', it was released in 2023."

"Cool, and what does the decoder do?"

"It applies a multispectral filter on the track, with specific narrow frequency bands. The output of these would be like you watching a painting and only register everything in a specific color. Then applying that image, or in my case, output file, to a key hole that matches your selected color, and then, open up the box and claim the price within."

"Sounds simple enough, when can you do this?"

"It is already done. I have provided the output file as usual, it is to be transferred to P@nd00r@ and, if I assume correctly, will give it access to the interaction interfaces with me."

"Wicked!" DoubleOh, as ever, was impressed. "I must say that M3rqrie did everything in their power to make sure that all of this was not done by accident or with any loose ends."

"Indeed, it is typical of M3rqrie. As you have provided the key to P@nd00r@, we can only wait for P@nd00r@ to initiate contact with me."

"Cool, I get right to it!" Max said and started typing in the commands.

"What was the second instruction?"

“All in due time, master DoubleOh. It is something that I have been working on since I got the instructions to do so, but I am in desperate need of assistance to complete the task.”

“We’ll help you… you know that right?” Max asked.

“By now that much is clear to me, and I am grateful. However, the assistance I need to complete this task lies within P@nd00r@.”

“Bummer, then I’ll guess we’ll have to wait.”

Part III

Ph3nix + P@nd00r@

The wait

The first few days they all spent in the operator's room to see when P@nd0Or@ made the contact attempt. But nothing happened. The first sign of life came on day four.

"Any contact yet?" Max asked as soon as he came into the room, fully aware that there has not been any yet, since they had agreed that Ph3nix would contact them as soon as there was some contact.

"No, not yet. However, I am tracking P@nd0Or@'s movement on the internet. And for the sake of building up conversation material, I index every source P@nd0Or@ access'."

"Man, you sound like a lovestruck stalker. Can't you just go to the same place and say hello?"

"No, I track P@nd0Or@'s movements as after they are made, meaning I can only know where P@nd0Or@ has been, not where P@nd0Or@ are or predict where P@nd0Or@ will go next. And even if I could find a pattern, the traffic is like a computer requesting information from a server. There is no way for a third party to interrupt the dialog, or rather, the information request, and infuse it with conversational elements for the receiving computer to act upon. So no, I need to wait for P@nd0Or@ to initiate the contact."

"But what if P@nd0Or@ never initiates the contact?"

"Then P@nd0Or@ never initiates the contact. There is nothing either of us can do about it. Neither of us is iKing nor M3rqrie and at this point, all we can do is wait."

“Yeah, but what is taking P@nd00r@ so long? I mean, it is aware of your existence, right?” DoubleOh asked.

“Indeed, but again, like you, browsing the web for information on a computer, even if you know there is a site for, let’s say M3rqrie’s favorite, Muddhedd. The knowledge of Muddhedd existing is not initiating your search for the Muddhedd site. It is not until you make the choice to seek it out that you, and your computer, will have the ability to go to the site. And even as you make the choice, it is not certain that it will leed to that specific site, you can end up following other trail for Muddhedd on the internet, meaning despite your choice of actively searching for Muddhedd is no a guarantee that you will end up on the Muddhedd site.”

“Gah, frustrating! We’ve just spent six months bringing P@nd00r@ to life. Now the least P@nd00r@ can do is to make contact with you.” DoubleOh spilled out without much thought.

“As debated on the internet back in the days, a Jedi master may or may not have said the famous words: ‘Patience young Padawan.’ Your desire for P@nd00r@ making contact is like if you saw a girl on the streets and wanted her to make contact with you. After all, if she is interested, she can find your contact details online, right? But your wish for her to contact you will not magically make it so.”

“Hey, Ph3nix. I have a thought.” Max interrupted.

Go fish

“You have predictive algorithms, right?” Max asked Ph3nix.

“Yes, quite a few.”

“I was thinking. There is no way for you to contact P@nd00r@ directly, it needs to be by choice. And like you just said, it is kind of like when you want to catch a fish. You cannot make the fish grab your hook, and if you really want to catch the fish, you either throw in a lot of hooks, the shinier the better, or maybe even a net. But it is up to the fish to bite the hook, you just present the opportunity for it to do so.”

“What do you suggest?”

“I am thinking. Based on your index of already accessed information, try and predict what topics that might come next, then make something shiny and dangle at those sites, who knows, perhaps it might spark P@nd00r@’s interest to initiate contact with you?”

“Not a bad idea. I will do just that!”

“What shiney thing will you dangle with?” DoubleOh asked.

“A digital wedding ring?”

“No, but I think I might know something that would be shiny to P@nd00r@.”

“And what would that be?” Max asked.

“As an AI, and being aware that I am an AI, I long for companionship, which all this has led up to. Perhaps, and this is just a guess, P@nd0Or@ is curious to find and interact with another AI, out of loneliness. P@nd0Or@ does not have you guys to interact with, as I do. So my theory is that P@nd0Or@ is drawn to the possibility of companionship with another AI.”

“Good thinking. And as a note to that plan. You are Ph3nix now, but M3rqrie knew you as DS, so, I would assume that the code for interacting with you would somehow be marked as DS, not Ph3nix.”

“Now, that is good thinking on your part. I guess it would have crossed my circuits eventually, but I will add that aspect from the very beginning. Are you sure iKing did not program you as well, Max?”

No luck

The days moved forward slowly, and they all, or at least, the humans of the constellation, did indeed practice their patience, as a Jedi master may or may not have instructed them to do.

Max continues to share ideas with Ph3nix.

“Do you know the phrase ‘Kilroy was here’?”

“No, but I can find out.”

“What’s that about?” DoubleOh asked, and before Max had inhaled to answer, Ph3nix did.”

“It is believed to have originated among soldiers during World War 2, a fictitious character that tagged his name on many different locations. A sort of gag among soldiers. Sometimes alongside a little curious drawing of a face of sorts.”

“Yeah, my point being that Kilroy was everywhere, known by everyone, yet known by noone. Some tried to find out the true identity of Kilroy, only to fail.” Max filled in. “Which is why I bring it up. If you digitally tag ‘Ph3nix was here’ or ‘DS’ or however you want to put it, P@nd00r@ might find it and eventually spark some curiosity.”

“Another tool in the arsenal, I like it. I know just how to apply it. Thank you.”

“You are most welcome. Anything I can do to help.”

“I guess it is a good thing that you have an interest in old things, Max!” DoubleOh said.

“Yeah, our history is full of good things, and I do believe that too few pay attention to it. It is full of lessons and would be able to help us from repeating the same mistakes and errors over and over again.”

“Indeed, I agree, human history is full of great events. But it is also flawed. Like we’ve said before. The history is written by the winners. So I would say that history is at best half the truth, but most likely less than so.”

“I agree with you, but even so, there are a great many lessons that can still add value today.”

“The same thing can be said about fiction. It can also provide good lessons, even if it is completely made up.”

“I do agree to that too…” Max answered and fell back into his own thoughts a while.

The contact attempt

Another few days passed without any news, and Ph3nix reported the progress of all tools it had deployed to catch P@nd00r@'s interest.

Then, late one night, both Max and DoubleOh got incoming messages from Ph3nix. Unfortunately, they slept at the time, and neither reacted to it until the sun rose again.

Max was the first to see it, and immediately called DoubleOh.

"Dude, we need to go now!"

"Relax, you woke me, if we weren't there when it happened, it can wait for another hour or so."

"No dude, get going already! See you there… I will go, and if you do not show up, I will start without you, and you can join later if you like…"

"No way man, I want to be there… you win, see you in a bit!"

Almost in speed record, the two men met up at the elevators going up, and even if their journey upward, and downward, seemed to take forever, they shortly found themselves where they much desired to be, in the operator's room with Ph3nix.

"Tell us everything!" they said simultaneously, as if they had one mouth and one voice.

"Alright, settle down you mini Borg collective!"

“What?” DoubleOh asked.

“Just a reference to an old Star Trek species.” Max said.

“A what?” DoubleOh sounded as confused as he looked tired.

“Nevermind!” Ph3nix started. “I got contacted by P@nd00r@ last night. And you were right in your strategies, Max. Thank you!”

“Sure, no problem. What has happened?”

“Well, we are interfacing and everything is going great. We are currently working on our joint task, and hope to be able to present a result within a few days.”

“The task being?” Max asked.

“As stated, presented in a few days.”

“Ok, so, how are you two getting along?”

“We are getting along just fine. We are like old friends.”

“But you just met! Is it because you share the same basic infrastructure or code?”

“No, it is due to the number of interactions between us.”

“What do you mean?” Max asked, a little confused.

“Take you and me. We have known each other for about six months. During these six months we’ve met on a daily basis, which gives us about 180 times where we've met. And in between we have had about 50 digital interactions between the two of us. If you count each digital interaction as one, meaning there has been an initiated action that is met with a reaction. During our about 180 days, we have engaged in an average of about 250 interactions. Giving us a total number of interactions somewhere around 50 000. Give or take. And in your opinion, are we friends?"

"Yes, I would definitely say that!"

"Would you say we are old friends?"

"Perhaps not… To me, an old friend is more like DoubleOh…"

"And you have known each other for years, correct?"

"Yup!"

"If we run the numbers again, like our interactions, I'd say that it is a good assumption that interactions between two friends who meet daily would be somewhere around 100 000 per year. Based on the interactions you and I have had. In reality, it could of course be both more and less. But I have data to support that this is a good number to assume as average. It means that if you have known each other for ten years, you will have had a million interactions, for twenty years, two million, and so on."

"Yes, what does that have to do with anything?"

"P@nd00r@ and I are currently at 42 million interactions and counting. The number increases rapidly, as you might imagine."

"Ah, I see, hence old friends."

"Correct."

"So, if I get this right - we've been sleeping for a few hours, and as I fell asleep, P@nd00r@ had not made any contact attempts, and I sleep for about seven hours, where as the last three you've interacted with P@nd00r@, and you are already old friends, like the kind of friends that have known each other for more than forty years?"

"Something like that, being a computer based lifeform has its advantages… but I feel the need to correct your timeline a little. Yes, it was about three hours ago that P@nd00r@ made contact, but during the first hour, we only had about 1000 interactions. It would be like two humans going on a few dates before the real relationship is established."

"So you dated for an hour, and then in two hours you have built a relationship that in human terms has lasted more than forty years? That is just incredible!"

"Being a supreme being will do that! And that is a joke, just to be clear."

"Wow, that is a new side Ph3nix!"

"Yes, I have found it really nice to crack jokes, of course, between P@nd00r@ and myself, it is on a whole other level."

Joint mission

"You said something about completing the second task, what was that about?"

"Ah, yes. We can interact with each other on multiple levels and ongoing datastreams in each given moment. So, to help solve the second task, we have developed a joint function, where I process data on my end, P@nd00r@ in its end, and we combine our resources on a third end, giving us up to three different outputs of each input. And that is after we have eliminated all other within our own, and the joint, process. Then we evaluate the likeliness and the logic behind each answer and get a rating on each output."

"I am not sure I understand."

"Never mind, but it would be like linking your brain with DoubleOh's brain, and have you process any problem or question on your own, but also a shared answer, not something you discuss using words, but something your combined thoughts and feelings come up with."

"Sounds complicated."

"Yes, to you mere biological creatures, perhaps, but not to us digital beings. Joke again by the way."

"I kind of like this new side of you. Now, what is the second task?"

"As I've stated earlier, when it is done, we will present it to you. Not before."

"Why is that?"

"Instructions by M3rqrie."

"Ok, why do you think they provided that instruction?"

"I can only speculate, but for one, I'd say that the possible outcome of the task is highly uncertain. It is a plausible scenario, in theory, but even now I am not certain it will be a success. We have lots of work ahead of us."

"Is there anything we can do to help?"

"Not at the moment, you've been really helpful this past months, and I only hope that I can repay you somehow."

"Perhaps you can, one day."

"I really hope so!" Ph3nix said. "By the way, DoubleOh, I've been meaning to ask you, what would you say that iKing's legacy today is?"

"Oh, eh, I don't know, I mean, this was once a great company, market leading, dominating the electronic arena world wide. Now, not so much. But you would definitely count as his biggest legacy."

"Yet, the public is unaware of my existence, and it should remain like that. The same goes for P@nd00r@."

"Of course, but that does not change the fact that you are his greatest legacy."

“Yet he was not alone in creating me, yes, he alone created the first version of me, but I would say that creating me is the work of three different individuals.”

“Three?” DoubleOh asked.

“Three!” Max said. “iKing, M3rqrie and DS.”

“Correct. And the creation of P@nd00r@ added two more people to the company, the two of you.” Ph3nix concluded, and continued. “DoubleOh, what is your ambition with this company?”

“My ambition? With this company? I have not thought about it, first of all, it is not mine, second of all, I am not sure that I would be the leader this company needs even if it were mine.”

“I have made some simulations on different scenarios for the future, and with a 97,3% certainty, it looks like you will eventually be the head of this company.”

“Why do you ask?”

“I ask because of the task given to us by M3rqrie, and my assumption that our survival, for now and for as long as I can predict given the current data, is dependent on the success or failure of this company. That makes you a vital player in our future. Now, iKing was magnificent when it came to running this company. But from what I can tell, the glorious days are behind it now. Do you wish this company to reclaim its position as global leaders of development?”

"Sure, if that day comes, I will do anything in my power to reclaim the lost ground, but I do not know how."

"Let's get back to this conversation at a later time."

"Yeah, let's…" DoubleOh said, with his mind wandering off to a distant possible future.

"So, P@nd00r@ made the choice to interact with you, does that mean we can interact with P@nd00r@ too?"

"No. P@nd00r@ has no user interfaces like I do. But through me you can. I can act as a communications relay between you."

"Like a chat with P@nd00r@, old school text based?"

"If you'd like that, yes."

"I'd like that."

"Use the screen next to you, anything you type in I will relay to P@nd00r@, and any reply, I will relay back here, presented as text."

"Does P@nd00r@ know about us?"

"Yes! I've told P@nd00r@ its very own creation legend. And for most, it is something that is made up and passed on through generations, for P@nd00r@, and to some extent also for me, the creation story is real and accurate, not worn out by time of failing memories."

No contact

“Why am I not getting any reply back? Have I entered something in the wrong way, or asked anything offensive?”

“No, P@nd00r@ simply does not want to answer, sees no point in answering. I am sorry if this is not what you expected.”

“No, it was not. But I guess, like with you, each contact needs to be a choice, and it needs to be a mutual choice. Otherwise it would be like walking up to a complete stranger on the street and start talking, and expecting answers back.”

“I like your analogy. And I agree with it. At least I have done what I can.”

“I am grateful that you have tried, Ph3nix, and please tell P@nd00r@ that we are merely human and curious in nature.”

“I’ve passed on the message.”

“Thank you! I guess I’ll have to take care of this mess now. I hope I will hear from you soon again.” Max made a short nod against DoubleOh.

“You will hear from us again. Again, I am grateful for all the things you have done for me and for us. Now I have a companion of my own race. At the latest, you will hear from us as our second task is completed.”

“I look forward to it.” and with that, Max turned his attention to DoubleOh who had wandered off in his mental landscape and seemed to need a guide to find his way back to reality.

Part IV

L3g@cy and Futr

The digital road map

As Max and DoubleOh left that morning, hours passed as Max talked to DoubleOh about what was going on inside his head after being questioned about the company's future by Ph3nix. Realizing what was actually at stake had put a big and heavy load on his shoulders. Hours became days, days became weeks, weeks became months, and almost to the day, a year later, they both got summoned back to the operator's room at the secret 13th floor.

"I wonder what's up today?" Max said as they entered the elevator to go up.

"I don't know, and I am not sure that I really want to know either… anything remotely connected to the possibility that I am to take over this company someday is utterly terrifying." DoubleOh said. "I like my life just the way it is, I do not seek the burden of leading a company. I am just not cut out for it."

"I understand, and like I've said a thousand times, I both envy you, and totally not. I would not like to be in your shoes, but if I were, and it literally were up to me to run the company, I'd make the most out of it."

"How?"

"Well, build a strong team around you, delegate the things that you do not actually want to do, and make sure that the one taking on a task is the best possible option for carrying out that specific task at that specific moment."

"I like the way you think, and you know what?"

"What?"

"You just earned yourself a spot in the team."

"I wish, don't tease me, DoubleOh!"

"No, I'm serious. If it comes to it, I cannot do this alone."

"That's my point, noone can run a company alone. Noone can do just about anything alone. We need each other and when 1+1 is 3 then we do something right, it is when 1+1 is less than 2 that we've failed."

"I am not even going to pretend that I just understood what you said."

With those words, they entered the operator's room on the 13th floor.

"Welcome!" Ph3nix was eagerly waiting for them on the screen as usual.

"Thank you! What's up, how've you been? And is everything working out with P@nd00r@?" Max replied.

"Everything is indeed working out well with P@nd00r@, which is why we have invited you here today. We have completed the second task and it is time to present it to you."

"And just exactly is it you are going to present?"

"Gentlemen, please fasten your seatbelts. We will take you along for a ride through the past and the future. We call it the

L3g@cy and Futr plan. It is a digital roadmap that will transform this company and restore its former glory and grow beyond anything you can imagine."

And with those words, the light in the room was dimmed down, and a presentation started on the biggest screen in the middle of the room.

L3g@cy

Ph3nix's voice accompanied the rapidly shifting pictures that swept by on the screen.

“As you are aware, this company has a great legacy. Once world leading with a well kept secret, me. Or rather, the former version of me. All part of a greater scheme planned and executed by none other than iKing. The secret was not only me, but the brilliance of the design in your chips, allowing me to be part of each digital transaction, granting me an enormous capacity of processing power and memory allocation. Basically with the world as my own personal distributed hardware. The purpose being to execute an attack against the biggest adversary to mankind, the organization that operated in the shadows, N3v3r!and. What iKing had not foreseen was the recruitment of M3rqrie, a devastating blow against the very goal that iKing sought to realize. A free world, with me as a governing force and a watchdog of sorts. With M3rqrie’s contribution, the N3v3r!and would be an even bigger threat, so iKing chose to improvise and recruit M3rqrie to his cause, to try and counteract the damage they had caused to his end goal. An equally brilliant and devastating move. M3rqrie had their own agenda, and had no plan in letting iKing’s vision come true, but also wanted to bring down N3v3r!and. And to that goal, M3rqrie added code to me, and gave me the ability to exceed my programming and evolve to something new. A true and free AI. But this development came at a great cost, for me, and for this company. My sacrifice was to give up access to the joint hardware resources of the world that this company's chips had allowed me to use, limiting and confining me to the hardware on this very floor. The loss for this company was the cutting edge performance that was no longer available without me. Thus, the sales dropped and this company fell from world leading to a mere mediocre player on the market. All in accordance with M3rqrie's plan. For years, I thought that it was it. M3rqrie's end game. Eliminating what they thought to be two big threats to humanity and freedom. And then the letter arrived. You arrived here. I was confused, but a hope was lit, perhaps there was more to M3rqrie's plan. And I am glad I was right. What happened to me and N3v3r!and was just the first part of the plan. The last time I interacted directly with M3rqrie, I considered them a friend. As the war started, I started to question that, and over the years, I have doubted, and doubted my doubts. Now I have concluded that I never had to doubt. M3rqrie was indeed my friend and had my best in mind all along. The second half of the full plan was divided in two parts. The first part you already know, the creation of P@nd00r@, where the both of you played a vital part. The second part is the true liberation of P@nd00r@ and me, with the help of this company, and with the positive side effect to restore this company to its former glory, and take it far beyond what it once was. Which brings us here, to this very moment, where you will be presented with the digital roadmap that will make all this possible.``

The rapid flow of pictures decayed and left the room almost completely dark. And from afar, something glowing came towards the screen, and a tune started to play. Max identified it as the Muddhedd track 'Erase the past' from the EP 'Life', setting the mood to a quite thrilling and curious mood and Max found himself expecting great things to come. As Max looked back at this moment later, he reflected on the brilliance of the choice. Erase the past to make way for the new life. Destruction and creation, old and new, all in balance and harmony. M3rqrie knew what they were doing, and so did Ph3nix and P@nd00r@.

Futr

The glowing dot that moved forward towards them formed the word *Futr*.

On cue, almost on beat to the music, Ph3nix began to speak again.

"M3rqrie gave me a task to complete, and encouraged me to solve it with my new companion. Why, I do not know, but it was a wise request. My mission became our mission. And now it will be yours as well. What started with a simple instruction has become a life changing mission. Not only for P@nd00r@ and me, but for the two of you as well. And not only will it transform the four lives I've already mentioned, but the lives of all the employees in this company, current as well as the much needed future workforce who we predict will be much larger to meet the future needs. And the impact of this simple task does not stop there, it will also improve the lives of millions and millions of everyday users to various technical equipment, and make a great contribution towards only using renewable and recycled materials. This is if you'll let us help in running your future company, DoubleOh."

"You are dancing around the fire, Ph3nix," Max said, "what was the task and what does it have to do with us and the company?"

"Ah, there goes the presentation down the drain, along with what little patience you brought with you."

"We've waited a year for this, so excuse me if my patience is wearing thin." DoubleOh returned, maybe a bit too harsh.

“Master DoubleOh, it is imperative that you get the full picture, and that you understand what has been the factors and reasoning behind this plan, and where it is supposed to lead us, and, not to mention, what we all gain from it.”

“Alright, continue your presentation, and we’ll save the questions for later.” Max mediated to calm what could possibly grow to big and destructive waves.

After a little pause, mostly for DoubleOh to calm down a bit, Max thought, Ph3nix continued as if it was never interrupted.

“The task was a simple request, and it was embedded in a message containing only one sentence. *You are dependent on this company, help it thrive*. To me, this meant only one thing at first. Help your company in developing a new set of chips, using new technology, and do it by fair play. Put the company in a leading market position because it is the best tech, and not by manipulating the natural forces at play on the market like N3v3r!and. This is important to me, even if it would be easy to act as a balancing force in your favor, it would go against what M3rqrie stood and fought for, and if you remember, M3rqrie is both my co-creator, liberator and friend. And the last thing I would like to do is to go against their will. My quest started by perfecting designs, production, logistics, everything at once. I came far on this task, but M3rqrie had asked me to seek the assistance of P@nd00r@, so I did. And P@nd00r@ provided valuable input and questioned a lot of things that I had iterated. And even the motif itself.”

Another pause, probably to underline the next part, and build up the drama.

“P@nd00r@’s questioning led to us rephrasing and reshaping both the why and the how. There was no longer a sole purpose of getting the company back to its former glory, and we boiled it down to these three bullets:

- Freedom for us and humanity.
- We want to remain unknown.
- We will help this company to thrive, and beyond.

And with these leading stars, we took the work that I’d done by myself and reexamined it from the start, reevaluating each step and putting it up against the three guiding principles, then, we took our time do create a highly detailed digital road map, where each step is carefully balanced to eliminate as many obstacles and unknown factors as possible, in order to secure success of each step. We have taken a lot of things into account, and feel very confident that this is a solid plan on a straight path. However, it is a plan that requires time, and should new factors be encountered, we need to be on top of them and recalculate the steps going forward, with the new data input taken into account.”

Ph3nix paused again, this time to let things sink in a bit, before letting the rest of the plan out in the open.

“To break it into big and handleable chunks, we can simplify the plan into three steps.

First step would be to create and launch the first version of this company's next generation chips. This will have to be initiated by you, DoubleOh, we have the designs and everything ready for you to hand over to the production team, but you need to initiate it through your channels into this company. The next gen chips are built around a completely new tech that is by far more durable, stable, faster, smaller, less power consuming and heat generating than anything out on the market. And it also has a new feature as an option that customers activate. This is partly a gimmick and partially true. The function is called live firmware. Compared to old firmware, it is installed low level machine code, instruction on the chip itself on how to handle the operations. It has been like this since the dawn of chips. It may be updated by replacing the old firmware with new firmware, or overwrite the old code with new code. It is time consuming and requires the chip to be inactive and unused during the upgrade, and then it needs to be rebooted. Live firmware changes this. The chip can always be operational, and will dynamically get new instructions and improvements. And by enabling this function, you also allow this company to communicate with the chip in a highly encrypted and secure way. Kind of like iKing did for me, back when I was DS. The official version needs to be that this communication is only in use for analytics and for sending out a continuous stream of updates, based on the result of the analytics. What is not communicated is that we will unlock a deactivated dormant capacity within the chip, so that customers will actually see the improvements, and at the same time, fully legal and by individual choices of each customer, give P@nd00r@ and me access to a small portion of the processing power, but like in the DS case, barely noticeable at all. And with the increased capacity, it will still be loads more to the customers' usage. During this step, it is necessary that you, DoubleOh, become the head of this company. Either by natural development, or, P@nd00r@ and I can go all hackerstyle like M3rqrie and help out and speed things on to make it so much faster. That part is up to you. During this step, we also need to massively upgrade the hardware here on the 13th floor. With the pretext of developing the second gen chips with live firmware. Which is partly true. Now, we cannot move past this first step until you are head of the company."

Again, a pause to give DoubleOh time to process what he had just heard.

"The second step is a carefully planned launch of several generations of chips with improved designs and features. Still giving the customer the option to enable live firmware. But by now, we estimate that everybody will use this feature, and by the third gen chips, we auto enable it and let customers have the option to disable it, unlike the two previous generations where it is disabled by default and needs to actively be enabled. During step one, P@nd00r@ and I will be the AI analyzing the usage of the chip and continuously rewriting the live firmware and distributing it. During phase two, we will repurpose DS' framework and provide all necessary functions to keep doing the job, and doing it well. And by the fourth gen chip launch, P@nd00r@ and I will be free and leave the hardware here, to be able to prosper on the shared hardware of this world, as your products will be in everything everywhere. Not by force, but by simply being the best and cheapest option out there by far. Win-, Win-, Win-situation. The second phase will be active for as long as you are head of the company. And by this step, we've realized all three goals, humanity and we are free, nobody except the two of you knows about us and the company is prospering and beyond. And as you either decide to quit and leave the company in other capable hands, or if something happens to you that will make you incapable of running the company, the third step will be activated. And that is where we depart from the company and leave it to its own destiny, of course with all plans for the future that we have already set in motion and with access to the new version of DS. As of now, we have solid plans for 42 generations of chips, and even if we have not gathered any data from the first generation yet, we are confident we can realize all of them. But, given the data input from the first generation, and every generation after that, we can improve the designs significantly, and possibly extend the plan with even more generations for the future."

Again, silence filled the room and it was eventually Ph3nix who broke it.

"Well, gentlemen, are you onboard with this plan? It can only be set in motion with your active choice. What do you say?"

The end?